SEVEN HAPLESS HOOPS

SEVEN HAPLESS HOOPS

BYRON JAMES-ADAMS

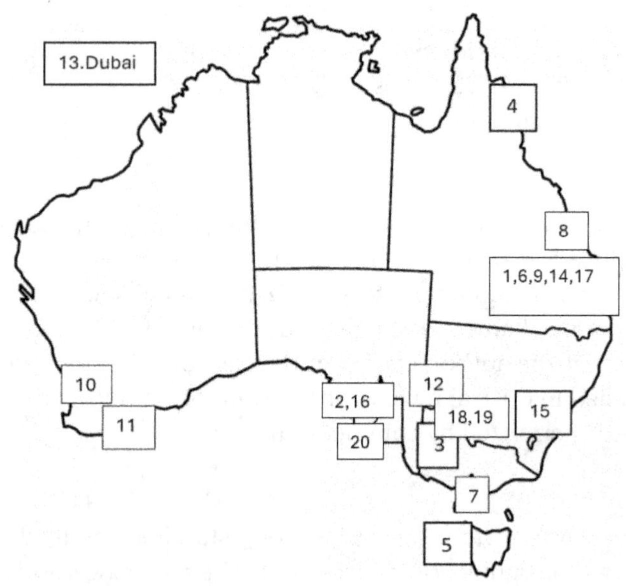

One Tricked Phoney:
1 Brisbane, 2 Adelaide, 3 Pinnaroo.
Two Hurtled Gloves:
4 Port Douglas, 5 Corrina, 6 Brisbane.
Three French Bens:-
7 Melbourne, 8 Rockhampton, 9 Brisbane.
Four Brooding Birds:
10 Busselton, 11 Margaret River, 12 Broken Hill.
Five Mouldy Bins:
13 Dubai, 14 Brisbane, 15 Sydney.
Six Geezers Lying:
16 Adelaide, 17 Brisbane.
Seven Hapless Hoops:-
18 Ouyen, 19 Mildura, 20 Kangaroo Island.

1

Rosemary Palmer was standing in the middle of a manure-filled horse stable chewing on the end of a bent straw, but unfortunately, it wasn't attached to the side of a margarita glass. Rose spat it out, sighed heavily, and rested her chin on the handle of a rake. 'Damn it, Sandy, this stuff stinks.'

Her BFF, Sandy Fraser, had just scooped the last shovel full and placed it carefully into a wheelbarrow. 'I know, and I still can't believe what we must do to get a dollar in our pockets. Life is too short for this type of crappy job.'

Rose was about to respond when their scam-busting associate and friend, Nic Thorn, ambled towards them formally dressed in an official Doomben Racecourse uniform.

Rose sighed. 'How long do we have to keep doing this, Nic?'

'Until it's done...then you can start in the next stable.'

Sandy looked at him. 'You're joking?'

'Nope...if I were joking, I would have said a horse walks into a bar, and the barman says, why the long face....' Rose leaned down, gathered a clump of soggy manure, and threw it at him, but Nic managed to evade the incoming missile, however, the man standing behind him bore the brunt of the lump instead. The man was wearing a white suit, a matching white trilby, leaning on a beechwood cane with a gold ferrule.

The man frowned and removed his hat. 'I guess I should introduce myself. My name is Charles Carrington, The Third, and I'm the President of K.P.I Events.' Rose collected a bucket of water and a sponge, then began to wipe the residue from the man's suit with her hands, but as she moved lower down his torso, he quickly grabbed her wrist. 'Sorry, Ms Palmer, I can't let you do that.'

Rose stopped, looked at him, and he added: 'The water is icy cold, it will make the suit shrink.'

Nic then stepped into the stable, gathered the rake and Rose's hand, and led her from the cemented pen. Rose brushed herself down. 'Have we finished yet?'

Nic nodded. 'Yep, but you'll need to move as the horse is coming back.'

Sandy and Rose stepped aside as the strapper led the horse into the stable. Sandy patted the rear flank of the magnificent animal. 'What's the horse's name?'

The strapper began brushing down the animal. 'No name.' Rose nodded. 'That's so sad...I thought every horse had to have a name. It forms part of the lineage.'

The strapper stopped mid-stroke, then nodded towards the lintel across the top of the pen. Rose and Sandy looked towards the wooden nameplate.

It read: 'No Neighm.'

Nic stretched and tapped the name, 'Yep, this is a Horse with No Neighm.' Rose nodded. 'That's a great song. Great band, too.' Suddenly, everyone and everything seemed to stop, even the horse appeared to go very still. Rose continued: 'I think the band was America. It was released around '71. Way before I was born.'

Nic smiled. 'Wow... I thought music and pop culture wasn't your thing.'

'It is when I need to know about stuff. We stuff our brains with only ten per cent of their capacity. There are some exceptions though Nic.'

'Thanks, Rose.'

'Nope, you dope. I meant there are exercises you can do to train your brain, and you can even put an app on your phone to keep your mind active.' Rose was about to show Nic an app on her phone when Carrington stepped further into the aisle and the horse broke wind. Sandy and Rose were not quick enough and were smothered by the invisible gaseous cloud.

Nic was standing behind them. 'Whoa...that's um...disgusting.'

Carrington nodded. 'Actually, it's a good thing. A healthy gut means a healthy horse.' Nic smiled. 'That's exactly what my Father says.' Sandy was taken aback. 'I thought you said you never mention family matters for personal protection?'

'In this case, I'll make an exception. Just warning you if you ever meet him.'

'Wow, so does that mean we are likely to meet him and the rest of your family?'

'Not likely.'

Nic noticed Carrington had taken a step backward, so he followed the movement and tapped Rose lightly on the arm. 'Guys, you might want to step back as there might be a second ...um...event.'

Nothing otherwise happened, and the young strapper held the horse by the bridle and turned the animal around to brush down the other side.

The horse's face was now pointed toward them, so Carrington took a cube of sugar from his pocket and offered it to the animal. 'She's a beauty, this one. I'm thinking of running her in the inaugural K.P.I. Events Cup.' Nic was about to respond when his phone rang; he held up his forefinger and moved away to answer the call. The group watched him go, and Carrington made another step backward, then held out another cube of sugar toward the horse. 'Did you get the brief?'

They shook their heads, and Sandy responded. 'It's usually a very brief...brief.'

Carrington was about to respond when Nic returned. 'Over to you, Thorn.' Nic nodded. 'What's up?'

'The ladies want to know why they are here.'

Nic smiled. 'OK. A long, long time ago, there was a big bang.'

Rose smiled, leaned down, collected some residual muck from the toe of her shoe, and then threw it towards Nic. 'Catch...,' and again, Nic moved out of the way and the clump landed squarely on Carrington's white suit. 'Damn you, Thorn.'

Rose looked at him. 'Hey, that's my line.' Carrington wiped the sod from his white suit and left the stables to head off for breakfast. Nic followed him with the bucket of water and the sponge.

Rose and Sandy began to move away when they decided to have a selfie taken with the majestic animal. Rose handed over her phone to the young strapper who reluctantly agreed. 'I'm not supposed to do this, but;' she wedged the phone between the rake prongs and extended it outwards.

The trio stood by the horse, and the happy snap was taken. The strapper nodded. 'I hope to have one of my own one day. I'd call it Alexa The Victorious, after me.' Sandy smiled and noticed one of the animal's eyelashes was white, the other dark brown, and the strapper noticed her staring.

Alexa rubbed the horse under the chin. 'She's only a filly, so the vibrissae don't match.'

Sandy patted the animal down its nose along the large, wide stripe. 'At least the white blaze matches the one white eyelash, and the front fet-locks match the white, too. What a well-colour-co-ordinated horse. Collars and cuffs.' Alexa shrugged and handed back the phone.

Rose and Sandy then left the stables and stopped in the restroom to change into something more or less suitable, sat down and ordered break-fast. Nic went to the buffet to start making the coffees and Carrington dipped his napkin in the pitcher to start wiping down the table.

'K.P.I. Events are a national group of like-minded investors pitching to operate annual social events to a selected group of participants. We offer horse and greyhound races and even organise a cricket match and a golf tournament. We also provide the stewards, the catering, and even the prizes. We co-ordinate the travel and accommodation options for the people to make it a whole weekend. It's a one-stop shop. Our inaugural event is in two months on Kangaroo Island, off the coast of Ade-laide.'

Sandy nodded. 'Good choice, as it's a beautiful part of South Australia.'

Rose took over. 'So, what do the local sporting clubs get out of it?'

Carrington hesitated. 'We pay them an event fee. Our group thinks this is the way of the future as it means we take care of everything as my people can run the entire event.'

Rose quizzed the response. 'But aren't you doing the locals out of a day's work?'

Carrington shook his head. 'Boy, you ask a lot of questions.' Nic had returned with the four beverages. 'That she does. It's not up to me to question the question though.' Rose continued. 'So, what does K.P.I stand for? I don't think it has anything to do with Key Performance Indicators.'

Carrington smiled. 'It's actually 'Keeping the Punters Interested.'' He was about to elaborate when his phone rang, but this time, he stood up and moved away to take the call.

Nic noticed he was nodding a lot and had turned his back on them. The call was disconnected, and Carrington walked from the room without saying goodbye. Rose watched him go. 'So what now seeing he's left us all alone?' Nic smiled. 'When in Rome.' Sandy looked at Rose. 'I think that means we are going to watch some horses run around the paddock.'

Nic tapped his nose. 'On the money, Sandy. Do either of you enjoy a flutter?' Rose shrugged and battered her eyelids. 'Do Melbourne Cup sweepstake count?' Nic smiled. 'Well, it's the big league here. Change it up.'

2

The trio moved out from the breakfast venue, stepped into the glorious Brisbane sunshine and moved to the parade ring. The first race was about to start and the strappers were leading the majestic animals through their warmups. Rose pointed to a small horse in the ring. 'I like the look of that one.'

Nic checked the name from the form guide. 'It's called "Larryn Jitis" It's just a little hoarse.'

Sandy shook her head at the name. 'Poor thing, maybe it should see a Doctor about her sore throat.'

Rose pointed towards another one. It stood at least sixteen hands high. 'Let me guess, that one is called "High-Horse?"' Sandy leaned over to read the name from Nic's guide. 'Nope. Getoffya-Soap-Box.'

Rose sighed. 'Do you know that the only exceptions to naming a racehorse is that the length can't exceed eighteen letters or be obscene, but that doesn't mean anything these days. I know of one called Horsey McHorse Face.'

The ten horses in the first field were then corralled toward the main arena as the race was about to start. Nic led Rose and Sandy to the betting area. 'I don't partake in the joy of betting but I've got some cash that's burning a hole in my pocket.' He handed over two one hundred dollars notes and Rose held it up toward the morning sun. 'We're not going to get done for passing bogus notes are we? I didn't think you liked dealing in cash, only giving credit where it's due.'

Nic shrugged. 'I'll go for a walk and have a chat to some people about which horses are known for winning, not whinnying. Please stay here and I'll see who is on the nose.' Nic returned a few moments later. 'I've got nothing. They're a careful mob these punters. We might have to hang around until eleven to see which way to go.' Sandy nodded. 'What happens at eleven?'

'The bar opens. They say loose lips sinks ships, maybe in this case it's good tips.'

Rose shook her head and joined the queue at the TAB. 'I'm going to put fifty on Larryn Jitis. It's got good odds.' Nic nodded. 'Yep, twenty to one.'

Rose stepped forward and handed over the cash and gave the betting slip back to Nic. 'Kiss it for good luck.' Nic licked the ticket and put it in his pocket.

The race was run and Larryn Jitis ran fourth. Nic pulled the ticket from his pocket and scrunched it into a ball, then handed it back to Rose. 'Maybe the horse reads The Bible. Go forth and multiply.'

Rose was about to drop the ticket into the nearest bin where the Race caller made an announcement. *'Ladies and Gentlemen please hold onto your tickets. We have a protest.'* Rose moved toward a group of punters watching the horses being led back through the yards. 'What's happened?' One of the group turned around and glared at her. 'They've called interference of the first three riders. Apparently they colluded to prevent the other riders from a clear run. Who did you put your money on?' Rose shrugged. 'Larryn Jitis.'

'One the nose or for a place?'

'I'm sorry, I'm new at this. I handed over a fifty and the bookie laid the bet.'

'Show me.' Rose handed him the ticket. 'It might pay a thousand. Hold onto it.'

Rose took the ticket back and headed back to Nic and Sandy. 'There's a protest on the first race. It will make it a long day. How long are we hanging around?'

Nic was about to respond when the caller confirmed the protest had been upheld. 'Until the money runs out.' Rose nodded. 'It will be a long day. I just won a thousand dollars.'

Sandy looked at her, then held up her betting slip. 'Me too. I took the same bet with the guy over there shaking his head.'

Nic shook his head. 'Crap. I was hoping we'd be going soon. How about you bet the other fifty on the next race, and we'll leave after that.'

Rose and Sandy nodded, then moved over to the TAB booth. They returned a few moments later. Rose held up her ticket. 'I've put it all on red.' Nic looked at the ticket. It read. "Lucille's Head" 'What about you Sandy?'

'I put mine on pink.' Sandy held up the ticket. It read "Bee More Like Alicia." Nic shrugged, and Rose leaned forward to explain. 'It's the singer's name.'

'Yep, I knew that but it's at a hundred to one.'

The race was run and Sandy's horse ran stone motherless last. Nic was looking up at the starters gate on the large television in case it hadn't come through as yet. 'I'm still looking for the horse, Sandy. Did it run?' Sandy smiled. 'It did. I heard it was its last race and is now being led out to pasture. What a way to go out.'

Rose headed off to claim her winnings and returned holding a paper bag and a big burly barman in tow. He had a tattoo that read " Beau" on his left foreman and the word "Bow" on his right one.

Rose held up her hand to indicate she had arrived at her destination. 'They wouldn't let me take the cash without an escort and have asked me to leave for my own safety.' Nic nodded at the man. 'Thanks mate, I'll take it from here. How much did you win?' Rose opened the bag to show them. 'I think it's about three thousand, plus the thousand I won before.'

Sandy smiled and also dropped her winnings into the bag. 'So why do they want you to leave?' Rose grinned. 'I told them punting on horses was easy and the guy behind me didn't like it.' Sandy continued. 'So?'

Rose shook her head. 'He'd lost over hundred thousand.' Sandy put her hand to her mouth. 'Just this morning?'

'No idea. He was the one that told me to leave and stop gloating.'

Nic smiled. 'Oh well, you win some and you lose some, but this is the last time I think we'll bet on a horserace. It's too stressful on the sods of grass.'

The trio ventured through the front gate and Nic noticed Carrington waiting for them. He walked over quickly. 'I've heard you are leaving. Good riddance to you all. Do not contact me.' Carrington then stormed off.

Nic turned around to face Rose and Sandy. 'That's not good as we may've been compromised.' Sandy looked at him. 'Does it happen often?'

'Not for a long time, somewhere in a far-off galaxy, but we may have missed out on investigating this scam or whatever this one is. We'll have to wait and see.'

Rose nodded. 'Will you tell us about the last time you were compromised? It wasn't with us, was it?'

Nic shook his head. 'Nope, it was only the one time, long before you came onto the scene. I've mentioned it before. It happened in Adelaide when Sister Gwen, the nun, not my sister. I don't think I have a sister called Gwen.' Nic paused to reflect on his sister's names, then continued. 'Anyway, Sister Gwen made a jump from a pedestrian bridge into the River Torrens. She's never been the same since. I liked it when she was a nun. There was none better.'

The trio crossed the road to head to the carpark when Nic noticed two nuns holding a sign that read. **'Betting is a Curse. Bet on Gods' Love.'** Nic moved over them. 'Good morning ladies, I understand that betting is a curse however I am wondering if you would accept a small donation to your cause?' He handed them the paper bag and didn't wait for their reaction.

As they were approaching the car Nic leaned down to collect a small, discarded box on the ground. He casually put it into his pocket, and as they got closer he noticed someone had written: **"Stay Away"** in red lipstick across the windscreen. Nic shrugged, 'Now that is disappointing,' then he opened the trunk and used a chamois to wipe away the warning. Meantime, Rose grabbed a towel to help. 'Why? Does it mean they are onto us?'

'Could be, but it's just it's such a lovely shade of red. What a waste.'

Nic wiped his fingers along the word 'away' and then rubbed it between the tips of his fingers. 'I would guess it's an Estee Lauder 'Restless' by the feel of it. It's not my favourite colour, I do prefer the 'Burmese Kiss.''

Sandy looked at him. 'Wow, I didn't know you were such an expert on lipsticks.' Nic nodded. 'Yep, I know them all: Red, Yellow, Orange, Green, Blue, Indigo and Violet.'

Rose leaned down to collect a discarded lipstick tube. 'I must say you've got good eyesight to read the small print without glasses seeing you're almost forty.'

Nic smiled, then extracted the discarded box from his pocket and Rose confirmed her suspicion. 'So, either Carrington has something to hide, or it's something else?'

'Could be neither, but it does mean we may have to step away from this investigation. I'll let my people know, but we still have this kidnapping thing, and there are always other things to keep us busy doing things. You guys haven't been to my family's farm to see the things they do, have you?'

Rose nodded. 'I almost did when we investigated that bottle recycling scam, and I almost met your sister.' Sandy grinned. 'Missed her by that much... I thought you didn't want us to know about your family.'

'True, but now, as you guys have messed up the opportunity for Nic Thorn and Associates to investigate the horsey thing, we'll have to find something else, and I'm not horsing around either.'

Rose grimaced. 'Please stop with the dad jokes. You're not qualified.'

3

They finished cleaning the windscreen, drove from the Doomben Racecourse, and headed to Sandys and Rose's home at West End. Sandy continued with the questions. 'So, who has gone missing? Surely not your sister?'

Nic shook his head. 'Oh no, she's safe...but one of her neighbours. Do you remember Wade Wilson and his wife, Julie?' Rose nodded. 'It was a little embarrassing when I drove onto their farm, jumped out of the car, then barrelled up to Julie thinking I'd got one over you and met your sister.'

'Yep, and they still talk about it years later. That's who called me.'

'Is it Julie or Wade that's gone missing?'

'Julie is missing, but Wade's mum was on the phone. Julie's car was discovered a couple of kilometres into the Mallee scrub. It was as empty as a politician's promise. Her bank accounts hadn't been touched, and her phone was still on the seat, along with her handbag. Keys were in the ignition.'

'How long has she been missing?'

'Only twenty-four hours, and that's why the local Police won't investigate it yet.'

'So, why did Mrs Wilson ring you and not Wade?'

'To remind me to RSVP to the Ouyen Primary School reunion invitation. They have demolished the school building. Such a tragedy.'

Sandy smiled. 'What's that? That Julie's missing, or the school was demolished, so there wouldn't be a trace of little tricky Nicky Thorn? Or that you forgot to respond to the invitation?' Sandy used air signals to emphasise "forgot".

Nic then used his hands to emphasise the entirety of his comments. 'All of the above, but it does mean we have to leave Brisbane to fly to Melbourne, then grab a puddle-jumper to make the short trip to Mildura, then drive to Murrayville.'

Rose shook her head. 'Please keep both hands on the wheel, and I hope you're not expecting me to fly in one of those bumpy balsa boxes with you. It's not that far to drive from Melbourne if we take a real plane.'

'Spoilsport. Tell you what, Sandy and I will take the puddle-jumper from Melbourne. I'll check for flights down from Brisbane. I should have enough points to make mine a free trip.'

Rose opened a flight website on her phone. 'It's about four hundred and fifty dollars to fly from

Brisbane to Melbourne, then you can take a regional flight to Mildura, and in the meantime, I can drive to Murrayville. All up around five hundred each to get us there plus petrol, plus the cost of a driver.'

Sandy nodded after making her own calculations. 'I'd agree with that.'

Nic continued: 'OK...but I'm paying and ...hang on ...I'm not paying. We can go commercial from Brisbane to Melbourne; then I can fly to Mildura for free. Something about someone that owes me something for doing something for nothing.' Rose shook her head again. 'I'm serious. I don't want to fly in one of those little paper planes.'

Nic smiled. 'How about a seven-seater?'

'Will you be flying it?'

'I could be, but it depends on whether I'm the pilot.'

'Damn you, Nic.'

The arrived at West End and were stepping from the car when a child went past them spinning a plastic hoop around her waist. It dropped to the ground, the girl stared at it, kicked it, picked it up and tried again. Nic smiled. 'I thought they'd banned those things.' Sandy looked at him. 'Children?'

'No...hoops...that's what they call the jockeys.'

Rose pondered the comment. 'Apparently so. It started in England during a National Racing Hunt about twenty years ago. One of the callers said, 'The jockey fell from the horse and cart-wheeled along the ground like a hoop', and it's stuck in the racing vocabulary ever since.'

Nic watched the child move away. 'Horses for courses, as they say. We have to leave ASAP as the first twenty-four hours make all the difference.'

Rose responded again. 'It'll take more than twenty four hours for us to get there.'

Nic smiled. 'And that's why I've already got my eyes and ears on the ground.'

'Who? Surely Wade isn't investigating the disappearance of his wife?'

'Nope. It's Driver and his brother from the same mother...Driver Two. They should be on the way and will meet us on Wednesday. We're catching a flight to Melbourne this arvo. I've already organised Dave to care for Dog, so all you have to do is pack.' Rose nodded again. 'For how many days this time?'

'Not sure, but at least a week or two.'

'Already done.... next.'

Nic looked at them. 'How? You didn't even know what was up.'

Rose grinned. 'No, but something is always up with you, and the only way we keep up is to make sure we're already packed up. Keep up, Nic.' Rose took a deep breath. 'Wow, speaking like you is exhausting.'

Sandy interjected. 'The only downfall is that we've had to have five suitcases already packed.'

'It must have cost you a fortune to be that prepared.'

Sandy grinned. 'Not really, we used your Business Expense Card. Thank you for our Christmas bonus, by the way.'

4

Nic began to reverse from the driveway when he noticed Dog in the rear view mirror and everyone knows you can't expect an eight kilogram cat to move out of the way in a hurry, it's just not done. Nic turned the engine off. 'It looks like Dog doesn't want you two to go quite yet. Have you fed him yet?'

Nic stepped from the car to pat the cat on the head and meantime, Dave, their next-door neighbour approached them and picked up the cat. Nic then patted Dave on the head. 'Thanks mate.'

Dave shrugged his shoulders. 'I guess that means you guys are off again without me. I'll look after Dog, otherwise he'll have to raid the local supermarket looking for tea and sympathy.'

Nic nodded. 'Shoplifting is not a good look for Dog, disguised as a cat burglar.'

The group then drove to Nic's apartment at Southbank, around ten minutes away and after Nic had turned off the alarm system.

Rose noticed it was a lot less tidy than usual. 'I'm sorry guys, the maid is on holiday, so I have to clean up after myself.' Rose and Sandy looked around the room. It was very unusual that Nic's place was untidy. Rose sighed. 'It doesn't look like a robbery. What's happened?' Nic nodded. 'Kids.'

Rose crossed her arms over her chest. 'You don't have any.'

'Not mine. My nephews and nieces, I can never tell them apart.'

'How many do you have?'

'I have no idea. There might be three, four, five or six. I've lost count.'

Sandy took a bottle of wine from the fridge and poured some glasses. 'Are you going to tell us which one of your sisters has the children?'

'Nup. I don't know myself. My sisters and the children all look the same to me.'

Rose shook her head. 'Really? Don't you think you should show more interest in your extended family just in case they need to rely on their Uncle Nic to get them out of trouble?'

'Nope. I've already taught them not to get into trouble in the first place.'

'Do you even know the children's names?'

'Of course I do. There's Marcia, Jan, Cindy, Greg, Peter and....um, Alice.'

Rose looked at Nic. 'You made up those names.'

'They're real people. I watch their home movies all the time.' Sandy shook her head. 'Really? They're the names of the Brady Bunch kids from that seventy's sitcom. I think you forgot Bobby' Nic nodded. 'That's the dog.' Rose interjected. 'No, Nic, the dog's name was Tiger.' Nic nodded. 'How do you know that?'

Rose continued. 'It's all part of the stuff I keep stuffing my brain with. Anyhow, what's for lunch?'

Nic rubbed his hands. 'We'll eat on the plane. I'll grab my stuff, and we'll head off. I've got to stop at my warehouse along the way to collect some other stuff.'

They didn't bother to tidy up.

5

Twenty minutes later, the group arrived at Nic's warehouse at Bowen Hills. The three-metre-high roller door was already open as he drove in. Nic nodded towards the detritus of papers and debris scattered throughout. 'Wow, it looks like the children were here too.'

Rose stepped out of the car and began tidying up. 'This wasn't children as they couldn't have tipped over the cabinets. Is there something you're not telling us?' Nic shrugged. 'I think someone doesn't want us to look into the horsey thing.'

Sandy went to the storeroom to get brooms and rubbish bins. 'Where are your warehouse people? I've just found Dee-Dee, but we should still call the Police.'

'It's all good. I already knew about it, and the Police don't need to get involved.'

Sandy started sweeping. 'But what about tending to Dee-Dee's injuries?'

Dee-Dee emerged from the broom closet into the main room, rubbing her wrists. 'Sorry, Nic, I didn't think they'd make such a mess. I told them I knew nothing, so all they did was put me into handcuffs and whip me with a horse crop.'

Nic leaned down, gathered a piece of paper, read it, balled it up and threw it across the room, where it landed in a rubbish bin. 'Three points and no net. It's all good, as there's nothing here worth reading, but it does mean one thing.'

Rose looked at him. 'What's that?' Nic shrugged again. 'It's time to find a new secret hideout. It's no point being Batman if people know where your hideout is.' Dee-Dee stretched from the residual tightness of the constraints. 'Hey, don't look at me. I don't do real estate, only computers and other secret stuff. Not that type of secret stuff.'

'That's OK, I've got a new place already. It's in the basement of the Police Headquarters on Roma Street. The only issue they'll have is the Batmobile being too loud.' Rose shook her head. 'Stop with The Batman stuff, Nic. You're more of a Flash ... in the Pan.' A woman's voice suddenly came from somewhere in the warehouse. 'Hey, that's not nice.'

The group looked around to see who made the statement, and an officious looking dignitary stepped from the shadows. 'Hiya Nic, this space will do. Are you leaving us all of the state-of-the-art computer equipment, too?'

Nic nodded and walked over to the woman to shake her hand. 'Sure. It's a good swap. My team gets space under your building, and your team gets access to my cyber-space.'

The woman nodded. 'Hello, Ms Palmer and Ms Fraser. I'm Deputy Police Commissioner Penelope Anderson, nice to finally meet you. Nic had told me so much about you both.' They shook hands, and the Commissioner continued, 'And please let me apologise to you, Dee-Dee. I was instructed to stay hidden in the office while they ransacked the place. Besides, I don't carry a gun, and wasn't about to call out 'Stop Police' as it may not have been ...um... appropriate.'

Dee-Dee nodded. 'Thank you, Ma'am. I had it all under control anyway.'

Sandy smiled. 'But you were handcuffed.'

Dee-Dee continued. 'True, but they didn't know I'd already released myself just in case they wanted to get nasty.' Dee-Dee showed her unshackled hands and tossed the handcuffs to Nic. 'Fifteen seconds. I think that's a record for me anyway.' Sandy nodded. 'Wow...I thought that only happened in the movies.'

'Nope. You hold the clip between your third and fourth fingers, guide the head of a paperclip into the keyhole, then use your thumb to turn the makeshift handle.' Nic shackled his hands together and held them up. 'Here, I'll show you.'

He stood there doing nothing so they waited and waited and waited. Rose grinned. 'You don't know how to do you?' Nic winced. 'A real magician can never reveal his tricks. Besides, there are too many witnesses, including a Police Commissioner.'

Commissioner Anderson looked at him. 'Go your hardest. I won't peek.'

Nic dropped his hands and raised them above his head; nothing was working, and the strain from the effort started showing on his face. 'Hey Penelope, I know you're not peeking, but do you have a key?'

Rose shook her head. 'Wow, something that Nic Thorn can't do.'

Nic took the key from the Commissioner and then handed over the handcuffs with the key. They were closed. 'Fifteen seconds, Dee-Dee, now that is a good effort. I think I did it in about two.'

'No way. How?' Nic smiled. 'Well, I'll let you in on a non-magician secret. If you don't lock the handcuffs, it's so much easier to unclip them.'

Nic then made a phone call to his other people to assist with the relocation process, and the Commissioner called her people to arrange delivery. There was a plethora of people to partake in the frantic packing party.

Two hours later, Nic, Rose and Sandy were chowing down on their in-flight snack of pringles and white wine heading to Melbourne.

6

The group landed in Melbourne, and their driver, "Driver", and his brother from the same mother, "Driver Two", were waiting for them at the airport baggage collection area. Driver was holding a sign: **"Nifty, Shifty and Thrifty."**

They shook hands, hugged and Driver led them towards the exit. 'We decided not to drive to Murrayville as we wanted to wait for further updates.' Rose smiled. 'What a shame, as that means I can come with you instead and not take up precious little space in a precious little plane.'

Nic nodded. 'Yep, that will work. I've arranged to collect a Cessna Skyhawk from Essendon Airport, so if you can drop us off there. I've already registered the weight manifest, I'll just change it.'

Rose nodded. 'Thanks, Nic.'

'Driver Two can come with me and Sandy, but he might have to lose some weight between here and Essendon.' The group collected the luggage, moved outside to the chauffeur area, climbed into

a Mercedes7 seater, and headed to Essendon airport. It was a ten-minute drive away.

Rose and Driver had said their goodbyes to the
others an hour later and were taking the six-hour
drive from Melbourne to Murrayville. Rose was
now in good spirits. 'I don't like flying.' Driver
looked over. 'And all along, I thought you didn't
want to be that close to my brother from the same
mother. Those planes only sit three, and it's still
a tight fit. I wonder how, um....Rog...oops, I almost
said his name...all of this Driver Two and Driver
stuff sometimes confuses me.'

Rose nodded. 'It has its moments, but what will
happen when Nic runs out of driver names? He's
used C.T. as the Cattle Truck Driver and Elle as L,
the Limousine Driver, but I have no idea how he
came up with your names...Driver and Driver Two.'

'Me either, and now he wants to use my wife,
Rita, for a job in Adelaide. Something about getting
access to a property and we discussed how easy it
would be to use Rita, disguised as a meter reader
for some surveillance work. She's already a meter
reader.'

Rose smiled. 'Lovely Rita, the meter maid. Hang
on, I forgot about Elvis, the driver. We met him in
Perth, coming out of a 7-11. Are we going straight
to Murrayville or stopping somewhere else? It's
about a six-hour drive.'

Driver continued: 'We're going to stop in Mildura. There's a Holden Motor Car Museum that we need to look at. Nic said we can stay overnight somewhere if needed, and I've even got a business credit card for the expenses.'

Rose nodded. 'Maybe we could buy a car from them and donate it back to the museum. I reckon Nic won't notice a four hundred-thousand-dollar transaction on the card for at least a month.'

Driver was about to respond when the car phone rang. 'This is Driver.'

'Well, fancy that, as I must have dialled the right number.' Rose interrupted. 'I hope you've landed. Planes don't have hands free.'

'It's all good; Sandy is flying it at the moment. We have about twenty minutes until we land. That's the hard bit, apart from crashing.'

Sandy joined the conversation. 'I'm not flying it. It's on autopilot.' Nic bounced back in quickly. 'Oh crap, I forgot to set it. Hang on, everybody.' Rose heard a manly scream in the background. 'Be serious. Are you joining us in Mildura or landing somewhere else?'

'Well, they've mown a paddock for me at the back of the Murrayville Police Station. I'll put this little bird down there if I can.' Rose overheard another little scream. 'How is Driver Two? Still with you?'

'He's a worse flyer than you. I don't think he's even opened his eyes at all.'

A gravelly voice came through the intercom. 'Are we there yet?' Nic responded. 'Not yet, mate, but we'll be landing soon. Just keep breathing and chewing on the gum. I've got plenty.' Rose continued: 'We're stopping at Mildura for a break as Driver wants to check out the Holden Museum. I've just Googled it, and they certainly have some fine-motor cars including a couple of Peter Brock's specials. I've always wondered where they ended up. We might have to stay over tonight.'

'Roger that.' The gravelly voice responded. 'Say what?'

Sandy interjected. 'Nic just said Roger that.' The man continued. 'Oh, I just thought you wanted me.... Oh crap...I'm not supposed to reveal my name, um...real name. It's not Roger.... It's um.' Driver blurted out quickly. 'It's OK, bro, as your name is not Roger That, so you don't have anything to worry about.'

Nic came through again. 'I'm glad that's all sorted. We landing soon. Bye.'

The call was disconnected, and Rose looked over to the Driver. 'So, is your brother's name Roger?' Driver shrugged. 'Well, sort of...it's his nickname. He spent so much time dressed as a happy pirate when we were growing up... so the family call him Jolly.'

'So, his name's not Roger?'

'Roger that. Actually, I have no idea what his name is. Good, we're here already.'

'Where?'

'Mildura. Didn't you see the signs?'

'Nope. I was looking for the River Murray. Let's get some lunch and head for the motor museum.'

They stopped, refuelled the car and drove over the Murray River bridge to the Motor Museum. A police car was in the car park with the blue lights flashing. Driver and Rose moved through the forecourt and arrived at the front of a large shed. It had a nameplate across the closed door:

"Work-Shed. Keep Car-m & Carry on."

The double-height roller door was closed, and a policeman rolled blue Crime Scene tape across the panel. Rose checked the situation. 'Something must be up as I don't think cop cars usually qualify as museum items.' Driver ambled up to him. 'I'll ask,' He reached inside his pocket to extract a Private Investigator license. Rose noticed and did the same. Driver held it up for the officer. 'Hi, I'm Driver, and this is Rose Palmer. We're here to investigate the theft of the car.'

Rose held her breath as she was unaware they were there in any official capacity.

The officer nodded, wrote their details down and pointed toward a small group of people standing by the museum entrance.

Rose looked over at the group, then back to Driver. 'I thought we were coming to look at the cars, not to look for a car that isn't there.' Driver nodded. 'Didn't you get the brief?'

'Nope.'

'Neither did I, but Nic must have, as he's sent us to have a little look.' Rose muttered under her breath. 'Damn you, Nic, I never thought I would use the P.I. thing. It was just something that Sandy and I were interested in.'

Driver stopped. 'You know in Australia, a P.I. has no real authority...it's more of a listening, taking notes and watching thing.'

'I guess so, and this will be the first time I've used it.'

'Me too.'

'So, what do we do?'

'Well...we start by listening, taking notes, and watching things.'

Rose and Driver approached the group, and everyone was very sombre. 'Hi, I'm Driver, and this is Rose. We're here to help.'

A woman with a name badge on her shirt read: 'Shirley' responded: 'Thanks for coming at such short notice. I was hoping someone would send someone. The local police are too busy to worry about this.' Rose nodded. 'We're here on behalf of Nic Thorn and Associates. What's happened?'

The woman was about to continue when suddenly, the sound of screeching brakes and a plume of dust encompassed the area. A young man jumped out of the car and approached them in a crumpled work shirt titled "Ronnie". He was trembling. 'Don't tell me. The Commodore is gone.'

Shirley softly rested her hand on his shoulder. 'You were supposed to drive it out of the main warehouse and leave it in the work shed for a service. What happened after that?'

'That's exactly what I did. You told me to take special care. I didn't even get it out of first gear. It's gone, and it's all my fault. I'm going to jail, aren't I?'

Driver stepped towards him. 'Which Commodore was it?'

The young lad looked up at him. 'And you are?'

'I'm Driver, and this is Rose. We're here to find it. Which car was it?'

Rose responded instead. 'I would assume that it's the last Holden Commodore built here in Australia and is reportedly worth around seven hundred thousand dollars.'

The lad looked at Rose. 'And?'

Rose continued. 'And actually, I assume it was the red SSV Redline that rolled off the Elizabeth line, in Adelaide on the Twentieth of October 2017, which you guys recently relocated from the

National Motor Museum in Birdwood in South Australia.'

The group looked at her, and Rose added. 'And I assume it's the only one missing.'

7

The man who appeared to be co-ordinating the situation called the police officer to their group. 'I think there's nothing more for us to do here today, just take a few photographs and everyone's name before you leave.' The Constable nodded and started to take pictures with his phone. Shirley added: 'Thanks, Barrie. Here's an employee list. It includes everyone who worked here in the last two years and our volunteers.' Shirley then provided a copy to Rose. 'Only a small team runs this place, and the staff turnover is low. We all love it here.'

They watched the plain-clothed man drive away, and a few moments later, the Constable followed. Rose leaned towards Driver. 'I bet this is an inside job.' The lad overheard and glared at her. 'There's no way it's an inside job if that's what you're thinking Ms Rose. I didn't catch your full name nor whom you work for.'

'I work with, and not for, a group of interested people that want to know how you lost a car worth over seven hundred grand.' The lad took a step towards Rose. 'I don't care whom you work with or for; this is well over your head.'

Rose stood at least four centimetres taller than the young man, and then he looked over to Driver, who had dropped his crossed arms from his chest. Driver was at least fifteen centimetres taller and fifty kilograms heavier.

Rose held out her hand, and the lad flinched. 'I'm Rose Palmer. We represent Nic Thorn and Associates. We are brought in to investigate scams, frauds, and genuine misunderstandings.'

Rose then referred to the list and found his name. 'So, what exactly do we have here then? Ronald Geoffrey Ayers.' The announcement of his full name took the lad aback. 'How would I know? The roller door was up. I drove the car from the museum warehouse and parked it in the work shed. I turned it off, left the keys in the ignition, shut the car door, walked out, and the roller door went down. That happened yesterday, and the car has been missing for twenty-four hours. Why has it taken you so long to start looking?'

Rose ignored his last comment. 'Where did you go after that?'

'Back into the museum.'

Rose looked at him. 'You know what I mean. Where did you go after you left the museum?' The lad took a step backwards. 'Do I need a lawyer?'

Driver took a step forward. 'We're in Mildura, not the U.S. Just answer the questions, son. The sooner we work out what's going on, the sooner we know what's been going on.'

'Huh?'

Shirley tapped him on the shoulder. 'They're not with the police, so you don't have to say anything, Ronnie. Just get back into your car, go home, and get dinner ready. Take the meatloaf from the freezer, defrost it in the microwave, take the veggies out of the crisper, and remember to feed the dogs. I'll be home in about ten minutes.'

Rose looked at Driver. 'I think we've been dismissed.'

Shirley overheard the comment and nodded. 'The police have gone, and unless you want a free tour through the museum, you two should be gone now, too.' Rose smiled. 'We'll be back tomorrow for a tour of the museum. What time do you re-open?'

'Surely you can't be serious. We won't re-open for at least a few days or when the police find the car. Our local Detectives are both on leave, so it'll take a couple of days before they start any investigation. Enjoy Mildura, and I'll be in touch.'

With that comment, the woman took off in a light jog towards the perimeter gate. 'And move your car so get can get out.'

Rose and Driver had only just made it through the gate before Shirley closed it behind them, and they watched as Shirley secured the lock. Rose sighed. 'Now, that wasn't the welcome I expected, and if the Detectives are on leave, who was the man running the show? He certainly looked like a cop.'

Driver nodded. 'And what's more, I suspect that Ronnie doesn't know how to use the microwave or he remembers to feed the dogs.'

Rose read through the list of names again. 'I'll call Chewy, our super sleuth, computer savvy and all-round geeky associate, to see if he can find out more about the names from the list.' Driver nodded. 'Should we call Nic first?'

Rose shook her head. 'Nope, no need. We can do this. Firstly, we'll find some accommodation and secondly, have some dinner. I'll call Chewy and then Nic, but I suspect he knows where to find us anyway.'

Rose called the Chewy, but the call went to voice mail: '*Aarrf, aaarf. You've called Chewy, and I'm currently out servicing the Falcon. Leave a message.*'

'It's me. I've sent a list of names. Let me know what you can.'

Driver smiled. 'That's not a very professional message on his phone.'

Rose shrugged. 'I've called him from my number, so that message is left just for me. I haven't seen any of those Star Wars movies yet, so I let him have his fun.'

'Great, I know what we'll be doing tonight. We'll just need a motel with Disney.'

An hour later, they'd booked two rooms at the Indulge Apartments on Ontario Street and sat at the bar waiting for a table. Driver was drinking soda and lime while Rose was on her second frozen margarita mocktail. The barman, however, was a little disappointed as he'd overheard them commenting on how much they could spend on their expense business cards.

Driver called the barman over to take another order. 'Busy night?'

'Yes, siree, mate. Tonight is the start of the Squishy Orange Festival, and we're booked solid for the week. I'm on clean-up duty later and have to go around the town with a bucket, mop, and much cleaning stuff. It's like that tomato-throwing thing they have in Valencia, Spain. The mayor thought it was a good idea as we grow Valencia oranges in Mildura, and they don't want them going to landfill.'

Rose smiled. 'Remind me to go to bed early then. What a waste of good fruit.'

The barman smiled. 'Oh no, the fruit isn't good. It's well beyond that.'

The barman then moved away to make another Screwdriver, and then the maître'd called them to their table. Driver waited for the waitress to take their orders, took another sip of his Soda, and then took a deep breath. 'Nic saved me, you know.' Rose looked over at him. 'OK, but I don't need to know about your history with Nic. He's very protective of keeping everything on the down low.'

'Yes, I know, but you and Sandy have been working with him for quite some time now. You should know what he does for...family.'

'I've got a pretty good idea that he'll keep us all safe no matter what we get into.'

'I agree, but what I will tell you happened about fifteen years ago.'

Rose nodded. 'That would have meant Nic was in his early twenties.'

'I believe he was. It also involved my brother from the same mother, Driver Two.' Driver hesitated, then continued: 'The four of us had just returned from our tour of duty.' Rose leaned forward. 'Four of you? You mean there are another two brothers? Driver Three and Four?' Driver stared into space, then returned to Rose. 'Not quite. Two of us walked off the plane, and the other two ....were loaded into a hearse. Our youngest brother and our sister came back in caskets.'

'And Nic had something to do with that?'

'No, it was well after that we met him. My brother and I were a little lost. No jobs, no home, and no hope. Dad died when we were all over in Afghanistan. He was in the service, too…it's why we all joined up. All four of us… We were used to handling guns, being under pressure and being organised, so we decided to rob a bank. Whether it was for the rush or something else, I don't know.'

Rose took a long sip from her straw. 'I don't need to know anymore.' Driver smiled but continued anyway: 'We researched the largest cash delivery day, which took weeks to assemble. I remember it like it was yesterday.' Driver then looked across to the bar mirror, held back his shoulders, and saluted at his reflection. "Hoo-rah'. 'So, when the day came, we parked across from the bank and waited for the armoured truck to arrive. It did, but it pulled next to our van instead of parking in front of the bank. It was too close. I couldn't open my door.'

'So, your plan failed unless you could get out the other side door or the rear?'

'As it turned out, another van pulled in on the other side. He'd reversed it into the space. It was so close that we couldn't get out on that side either. We tried to get the guy's attention, but he ignored us. He had something in his hand, a pipe or a metal bar, and then he disappeared behind the back of our van. We were watching him in the mirrors.'

'You could still get out via the rear doors.'

'So we thought, and we climbed back through the van and tried that, but they were jammed shut for some reason. We even used our boots against the panels, but they wouldn't yield.'

'So, what happened? Did you give up? Did you get arrested?'

Driver took a swig of his drink and continued: 'By then, we'd resigned ourselves to not robbing the bank, so we returned to the front seats and waited it out. The van moved away, then the armoured truck, and we sat there wondering what could have been.' Rose whispered. 'What happened then?'

'We saw a business card attached to the front windscreen under the wipers, so I stepped out, collected it, and sat back in the van. It read: 'Don't do this. Call me.'

Driver leaned forward, pulled his wallet from his pocket, retrieved a laminated business card, and handed it over. It was yellowed with age and had Nic Thorn & Associates on one side with a phone number on the other. Rose rolled the card through her fingers and handed it back. 'You've kept it for ...about fifteen years?'

'Yes, and whenever my brother and I think about doing something stupid, I pull the card out and talk where we could've ended up if Nic hadn't stopped it. To this day, we still can't work out how we knew what we would do. We called him, and he organised for us to meet with professional people to talk through our grief and then got us into the Army Reserves. Jolly joined the Victorian Country Fire Service and is high up there now. We now have families, and we all go to Geelong every Christmas to spend the Festive season with our Mother.'

Rose nodded and raised her glass, and Driver continued. 'On that note, I'm heading off to bed if it's OK with you. We can catch the Star Wars movies some other time. I'm going to call Rita and my boy.'

Driver stood and exited, so Rose called her parents, but it went straight to the message: 'Hi, Father. It's Rosemary...just ringing to say thanks for everything.' She disconnected, and after a couple of moments, her phone rang. It was her mother: 'What's happened, Rose? What have you done this time? You're on speaker. Your Father is here too.'

'Nothing, Mother. Hello Father. I just...it's time we put things behind us. I've come to terms with you wanting me to be married off when I was nineteen to save that business deal. It's been over ten years now. I'm about to turn thirty and think we should all move on.'

Her Father responded: 'That business deal was never going to happen, and we always knew your Michael Bush wasn't related to the Bush family of America as there was no way one of them would have so eagerly accepted you as their betrothed.'

Rose shook her head, took another deep breath, and continued the conversation. 'Anyway, I'm safe and happy and will still be around somewhere if ....' Rose couldn't think of anything else to say.

'Are you still there, Rosemary?'

'Yes.'

'OK...if you have nothing else to say, we'll hang up.'

They disconnected and Rose then tried to call Nic and Sandy, but they both went to the message bank. Rose put the phone down and muttered: 'Doesn't anybody want to talk to me?'

A well-dressed woman overheard and sat down in front of her. 'I'll talk to you, young lady.' The woman appeared to have a bodyguard, or at least someone looking suspiciously like one: dark glasses, blank expression, and built like a brick shiphouse.

Rose responded softly. 'I'm sorry, but I don't know you.'

'Well, my name is Della Ayers, and I'm the Mayor of this little town. I don't know you either, so we're off to a good start. Welcome to Mildura. Please enjoy the Squishy Orange Festival. I love the smell of rotting oranges in the morning.'

Rose stood, shook her hand, and offered her hand to the attendant, who ignored the gesture. 'Well, I'm Rose Palmer with Nic Thorn and Associates. We've been called in to investigate the theft of the Commodore out at the museum. Have you heard it was missing?'

'Yes. Nothing much gets past me. Besides, you would have met my better half there, Barrie. He's the sheriff here in our little town. He called me just as he left the museum and told me about you two. I believe you met my son, too, Ronnie, he lives with us. Anyway, I can't stay, just thought I'd say g'day…. Hey, that rhymes…Call me if you need anything.' Della handed over her business card. 'This is my mobile. The second number listed is Barrie's.' Della hesitated. 'Oh…and this is…she's um…my Bodyguard.'

Rose read the card. 'Thanks, Della …um…I hope we get the fella.'

Rose watched them leave and searched Google: 'Victoria - Sheriff' to confirm her suspicion that a Victorian sheriff is responsible for executing arrest warrants and not attending to investigations of a theft of motor vehicles, despite their value. She was correct. Rose settled the bill and stepped outside into the cool air, where the pungent aroma of rotting oranges was already enveloping the night. In the reflection of the shop window Rose noticed a car door open and shut. A man dressed in a dark suit lit a cigarette before making his way over to her.

'I've heard you're looking into the theft of the Commodore.'

Rose sized up the situation and presumed she would be safe despite being alone. 'Yes, I am. We are.'

'Well, I'm going to tell you something for your own good. Don't. I suggest you leave it to us.' The man handed over a Business Card. It read: "Vizinary Security"

'I'm Hanson Fonteyn, and we already know about it. So, stay away.' He then collected a discarded orange from the footpath, squished it in his hand, and dropped it onto her shoe. 'You have been warned.'

8

Around three hours earlier and two hundred kilometres away, Nic was bringing the plane in for a landing. 'Er guys...forget what I said about the landing strip as they forgot to mow the paddock, so it may get bumpy. That's the bad news; the good news is they remembered to shift the cows.' Nic lined the Cessna up as best he could and prepared to land. 'Hang on.'

Driver Two called out from the back. 'There's nothing back here to hang onto.'

'Well, I'll let you know when you can open your eyes.'

Nic throttled back, brought the plane to stalling speed, touched down, and bounced along for about two hundred metres. 'Can I open my eyes now?'

'Yep.' The plane came to a stop, and they climbed out. 'That was one of my best landings, I reckon.' Driver Two called back. 'Maybe for you, but I'm with Rose, there's not enough room back here. I prefer my planes to have overhead luggage compartments, drink trolleys, two pilots, and a barf bag handy.'

Meanwhile, a man approached the plane and started securing it to the ground. 'Good landing, mate. Sorry, I forgot to run the tractor mower over the strip. I got busy shifting the stock and then forgot why I was shifting them in the first place. I've got the car waiting for you in the woolshed as requested.'

A few hours later, Nic, Sandy and Driver Two were gathered around a roaring brazier outside Wade's farmhouse. Discarded packets of marsh-mallows littered the ground, and Wade was fussing about keeping his dogs away from the roasting lamb and the empty marshmallow packets. 'It's nearly ready, sorry it took so long. I'm not a cook. Julie did all the homey stuff. I do the farmer stuff.'

Sandy looked at him. 'Everybody knows a bar-b-que is a man's domain. Where were you when they were handing out the book on men?'

Wade shrugged and removed his gloves; his hands were covered with dirt and callouses. 'Doing farmer stuff.' Driver Two stood up and stretched, and Nic looked up at him. 'You seem to have recov-ered from our little flight?'

'And I'm looking forward to returning once my brother arrives.'

'Um...sorry, but they've got another job in Mil-dura, so we might be flying back... unless....'

'Unless what?'

'Unless it takes longer for us to find Julie than they solve the mystery of a missing motor car. I'll ring them in the morning to see what's what.'

Wade started to serve the meal. 'I hope no one is a vegetarian, vegan, or fussy fruit muncher.'

Sandy put her hand up. 'Sorry, I am a veggie. I should have told you before. Do you have any salad?' Wade looked at her, horrified. 'Salad, the only salad I have is the lupins. We feed it to the farm stock. I could find some other green leafy stuff in the paddock, like Lantana, Salvation Jane, or some tasty straw. Otherwise, keep eating the marshmallows.'

Driver Two then held his hand up. 'Sorry, I'm on a "No White Diet" so I don't eat anything white, like white bread, potatoes, or chicken. I'll do eat other colours though; a Rhode Island Red is my favourite. I drink white wine occasionally.' Nic then put his hand up. 'Sorry, Wade. I have something to confess, too. I only eat red meat, and it looks like you've cooked it too long, it's charcoal.'

Wade slumped down into the deck chair. 'No wonder she's left me. I can't even cook. I make a good brew of beer. Anyone for another?'

A fresh round of drinks was handed out, they rattled stubbies and Driver Two continued to glug from his water bottle. 'I'll keep passing on the beer as I have to drive these guys back to Murrayville later. So, Wade...do you know where she's gone, if she's gone, and if she's coming back?'

'Nope.'

Sandy shrugged. 'Did she say anything about leaving?'

'Nope.'

Nic downed his beer and started chowing down on a leg of lamb; 'You know there's no evidence that she's been abducted by aliens, so that's a good thing.'

'Nope...oops, I mean yep.'

Wade then stood up and stretched. 'You know what we're missing here?'

The group simultaneously responded: 'Nope.' Wade grinned. 'Music. I've been learning the guitar and have a captive audience. How good is that?'

Sandy looked at Nic. 'How long have you been learning the guitar?'

Nic smiled. 'About twenty-five years, and I'm still learning.'

Wade excused himself and headed inside his house. Driver Two looked over at Nic. 'So, what's your take on what's going on?'

'I suspect Wade doesn't quite know how to play the guitar.'

'Not about that. This missing wife thing.'

'Oh, that. Well, in the morning, we'll drive to the site where the car was found. Apparently, it's still there, but they need a tractor or a truck to retrieve it, and hopefully, the overnight rain hasn't washed away any tracks or clues.'

Wade returned with a guitar and propped himself on a tree stump. 'I know about five songs, but my best is 'Kumbaya'. It makes my job as a Scout Master much easier when I can play and sing this one for the cubs.' He started playing but struggled with the three-chord song. 'Damn, it's not supposed to be this hard.'

Sandy leaned over and placed her hand over the neck of the guitar to stop him from continuing. 'Whose version are you trying to do?'

Wade stopped singing. 'Is there more than one version?'

Nic nodded. 'Yep, there's a Peter, Paul, and Mary version. It's in the key of C or The Seekers version. It's in D.'

Wade was horrified. 'I only know this version. It's in the key of me.' Wade re-tried to find the tempo and then started again, but the dogs began to howl, so he stopped. 'You know that's the same reaction I get from the dogs every time I play. It's very distracting.' He put the guitar down but had to pick it up quickly as two dogs looked like they were about to use it for something else. Wade wiped the dust from it and then glanced at Nic. 'Do you still play?'

'A little.' Nic took the guitar, re-tuned it by ear, and played a version of the classic Led Zeppelin song "Stairway to Heaven". Wade beckoned Nic to hand back the guitar once he'd finished, then promptly took it inside.

The group waited for him to return, but he didn't, so Sandy stood up and started collecting the discarded rubbish and feeding the leftovers to the dogs. 'I think that's something else that Wade doesn't do. Play nicely. Do you think we should leave?' Driver Two stood and stretched. 'I agree. It's getting cold, and the fire is going out. I suppose he's expecting us back tomorrow?' Nic nodded. 'I guess so.' They returned to the car and drove back to the Murrayville Hotel.

It was early in the morning when Nic called Rose back. The call went through to message, but Rose immediately called him back. 'You didn't call me last night, Nic. Are you, Sandy, and Driver Two OK?'

'Yep. We've been busy, plus we've been out of range in the outback. What've you found out about the missing car?' Rose continued: 'It's quite an interesting case. I'm not sure what's going on, but when we arrived, it wasn't the police in attendance; it was a Sheriff. I assume to serve a warrant to someone, but we didn't see anything handed over.'

'I can get Chewy to search the court records to see who the recipient was.'

'I've already organised him to do that and have sent him a list of all those working at the car museum. When did you hear about the theft? You could've given us the heads up.'

'It was only a rumour. Chewy picked up some online chatter about a classic Commodore that would be available for sale. He somehow tracked it down to that one. Don't ask me how.'

'That's OK, I'll ask him. How are you going with the kidnapping thing?'

'It's weird. Wade has been a little odd about it, almost to the point that he doesn't care what's happened to her. He's given us the impression that he's been too busy farming to worry about ...um...coddling.'

'Have you spoken to his Mum yet?'

'That's first on the agenda this morning. We're meeting her for breakfast.'

'She's not on the farm next door to your sister?'

'Nope...Wade runs both properties now. She retired to the big smoke.'

'Melbourne or Mildura?'

'No, to Murrayville.'

Rose shook her head. 'Does your sister still live on a property next door?'

'It depends on what you mean by next door. Properties out this way are bigger out here. Bigger than most of those European countries.'

'So, what's out there?'

'Not much...we're way beyond the black stump.'

'Be serious, Nic. Oh, by the way, I spoke to my parents. I mentioned I was happy, and they didn't react. So much for wanting your children to be happy.'

'At least your brother is. Living in Hawaii, living the dream.'

'Yes, and I'm here in Mildura. Did you know it's the Squishy Orange Festival?'

'Yep, and you know what they say: when life gives you lemons, make lemonade.'

Rose responded quickly. 'They only grow oranges in Mildura.' Nic smiled. 'Well, make a screwdriver then. I've got as go, we're meeting Mrs Wilson for breakfast.'

They disconnected, and Rose began to review the names on the list and backgrounds as Chewy had provided the details overnight, however, the conversation with Hanson Fonteyn was still troubling her.

Back in Murrayville, Nic, Sandy and Driver Two were squashed together on one side of a booth inside the Cobb & Co. Café, waiting for Mrs Wilson. They were struggling to drink their coffees as it tasted of dirt.

Nic put his mug down. 'You know this is the best coffee I've had today.' Sandy responded quickly. 'It's the only coffee you've had today.'

'Thanks for pointing that out. Oh, and here comes Mrs Wilson.'

A woman of indeterminate age bounded towards them, holding a coffee pot. 'It looks like you guys need a refill. This is my brew. What do you think?'

Driver Two stood as she approached them. 'Nic mentioned it was his best coffee this morning.' The woman grinned broadly and re-filled Nic's cup. 'And they tell me it tastes like dirt. What do they know?'

Sandy muttered under her breath. 'Oh, they know, they know.'

Mrs Wilson sat down opposite them and beckoned Driver Two to sit beside her. 'Wow, you're a strong one, aren't you? Are you married? Are you taken?'

Driver Two smiled and said nothing. 'Well, can I at least guess your age? There are lots of single ladies in Murrayville are looking for a nice young man.' Driver Two smiled. 'I'm not that young.' Nic nodded. 'I can vouch for that. You're only as young as...I've no idea.'

Mrs Wilson continued. 'OK...would you let me read your palm? I do that sort of thing, and it might even help us solve the mystery of Julie's absence.' Driver Two looked at Nic, shrugged, and allowed Mrs Wilson to take his hand.

'My, my. I would say you're about fifty-three. You're married with two children. You live in a seaside suburb of Melbourne... and spent a few years in the Armed Forces...based in Afghanistan. You...well, that's about it so far. Sorry, but you've got coffee grounds on your fingers, so I can't read the rest.' Driver Two withdrew his hand quickly, and Mrs Wilson looked at Nic. 'How did I do?'

'That's quite an achievement. Please remind me to review Driver Two's online profile. I assume you've found him on Linked-In.' Mrs Wilson smiled. 'Actually, it was a Victorian Fire Safety and Rescue site. I thought I recognised him when you filled up at the B.P. I was in the bottle shop next door. His name is 'Deux' Driver; it's French for two.' She looked at Sandy. 'What do you want to know about Nic then?'

Nic held out his palm, and Mrs Wilson took it and rolled it over. 'Um...he works too hard and needs to find a nice woman to settle down with.' Sandy smiled. 'Is that all?'

'Not quite. His sister wants to know if he will visit her in Murrayville.'

Nic shook his head and withdrew his hand. 'That's not in the lines on my palm.'

'No, but I had to ask. Shall we order breakfast and discuss tracking down the allusive Julie Wilson?'

The group nodded, and breakfast was served about fifteen minutes later. They'd all ordered it to come with a pot of tea. Mrs Wilson took a bite of her toast. 'She's gone missing before, but it feels different somehow this time. Wade is a little ...um...shall we say a little indifferent about his life partner. He prefers the animals as they can't talk back. He would've got that from Herb, his Father; he didn't know how to keep me ...um...Well, we had a good five years of marriage. We were married for twenty-eight but had at least five good years. It went downhill when Herb couldn't ...well, he could, but his heart wasn't in it anymore.'

Sandy put her hand on her arm. 'I assume you're referring to lawn bowls.' Mrs Wilson nodded. 'Yes, let's call it lawn bowls.'

Nic smiled. 'So, how about Julie and Wade...how was their lawn bowls?'

Mrs Wilson shook her head. 'I think they've given up on playing; at least, that's what Julie has told me. They were playing lots of lawn bowls just after they got married, hoping for a...um...what's the little white ball they roll down first called?' Sandy nodded. 'A jack.'

'Oh, that's right. They tried for the jack for a while but found out, um...Wade's ...um, bowling action didn't quite...'.

Driver Two interrupted. 'You're talking about sex, aren't you?'

'Yes...but let's not talk about it in here. I'll grab a bag of coffee beans to go, and return to my place. It's just across the road.'

Nic and Sandy stood up, settled the bill, went outside, and waited to cross the road. Mrs Wilson checked for oncoming cars. 'We'd better wait for the traffic.' Sandy looked down the street where a car was coming slowly down the road about two hundred metres away. The vehicle had multiple rods and reels attached and turned into a street without indicating. The car tried to reverse back out of the road it had just turned down. The driver hit the kerb, stopped, and waited.

Mrs Wilson sighed. 'He drives by braille, old Maxie, can't see for looking. I don't know how he keeps his licence, but he probably doesn't have one anyway.'

The group crossed the road and entered the house. It was a new build, albiet in the 1970s, and out of place in the street compared to most others built around the turn of the century. They sat around the kitchen table, and Mrs Wilson continued: 'There's not much fishing around here apart from Dawson's Creek, but that only flows when it rains.' Sandy nodded. 'It rained last night.'

'Yes, it did, and the night before too. It's been raining cats and dogs for the last week, so that's where he's most likely been today. Sometimes you can catch Murray Cod or Red Carp, but most likely the only thing you catch is a cold.'

Sandy was reviewing an overhead photograph of Wilson's properties. 'The river runs through your property, doesn't it?'

'Yes...and I can show you where Julie's car is. It's not on this picture, though, as these were taken years ago before Wade took it over.' Mrs Wilson leaned forward to point at the area when a little white dog suddenly jumped onto the table and left a stuffed toy. Mrs Wilson patted the dog and then put him back on the floor. 'Good boy. Now go and annoy 'Poopy' instead.' The dog gave a little woof and took off towards the front door, where it jumped up until it turned the knob and let itself out. Sandy was impressed. 'Our cat doesn't open doors. It just wails until someone lets it out.'

'What type of cat?'

'Maine Coon. It's about ten kilos. We call it 'Dog.''

'Well, we called this little fellow Brian. Herb was a massive Beach Boys fan. Oh, by the way, 'Poopy' is the two-year-old living next door. All it does is poop. I can't wait for him to attend school when he's old enough.'

'Puppy school?'

'No, why would they send their boy to puppy school?'

Nic rolled up the map. 'Let's get this show on the road. We've been told they haven't salvaged the car as yet.'

'Nope. It's still stuck like a pig in ...anyway let's take my truck. It needs a run.'

They moved into the backyard and were directed to wait for the truck to exit the garage. The truck was a bright blue Toyota Hilux Dual Cab, and Mrs Wilson could barely see over the steering wheel. The sides of the rear tray had been removed, and a sizeable checker-plate tray had been attached instead. The licence plate read: "Dadstruck". Sandy noticed the license plate. Rose told me about this.'

Nic nodded. 'Yep, the old Bedford must've finally died.'

The truck chugged from the shed, and they all climbed in. Mrs Wilson struggled with the steering wheel against her ample bosom and being a stick shift, she couldn't coordinate the clutch with the gears. Every time she changed, the truck groaned, and gears crunched.

Finally, Driver Two had had enough. 'Can we stop, please? I'll drive.' The truck lurched to a stop. 'Sure, I can't handle the stick anyway.' They swapped drivers and started again. 'Where are we headed?'

'Back to the farm, we take a right to follow the track along the river. Big Blue will take it in its stride.'

They arrived at the farm and headed along the river track, but while the truck handled it quickly, the springs in the seats were well-worn and offered little comfort and they bounced around like kangaroos loose in the top paddock.

Sandy called out above the din. 'When was the last time you were up this track?'

'I don't come up this way very often as the track gets too close to the riverbank, and there's a likelihood we might go for an unwanted swim.'

Sandy continued. 'How far away is the car?'

'Another ten minutes' drive, then it's a ten-minute walk to the car.'

Driver Two expelled a grunt as they dropped in and out of another pothole. 'What type of car are we looking for?'

'A Daihatsu Charade.'

Driver Two grunted again trying to keep control. 'It would be quite an achievement to drive it through here.' Nic called out from the rear seat. 'Not unless you either towed it behind a tractor or put it on a flat-tray truck...something like this.' Mrs Wilson turned around to face him. 'Why would someone do that?'

Nic smiled. 'To make it appear that they wanted to disappear or if they had been abducted by aliens.' Mrs Wilson nodded. 'I guess so. We do get crop circles around here.' Sandy called out. 'Could Julie drive this truck?' .

'Of course, she could do anything my lazy boy Wade could do. He did make the tray-top for the back of this truck. It raises tips and everything and makes it easier to unload the hay when you feed the stock yourself.'

Driver Two found a safe place to park the truck, and they climbed out. It was close to the riverbank, so they looked at the flow below them. Mrs Wilson was the first to speak: 'The river's deep here. Can get up to about two metres in places when we get the rains, and at its widest is about three metres.'

Nic nodded. 'Deep enough for a canoe or a kayak.'

'I suppose so. I don't go much for that river stuff. I don't like to get wet.'

Nic smiled as it is something Rose often says to him, although Nic recently discovered Rose was previously a State champion surfer. 'Did Julie have access to a canoe?' Mrs Wilson continued. 'No idea, but a place in town hires them out when the river flows. It's an honesty system. You use it and put it back.'

'Are there any missing at the moment?'

'I don't know; it's not something I notice.'

Sandy looked towards the track and considered the trek they were about to undertake. 'If it's a twenty-minute walk from here. How would the car have been driven in so far?' Nic responded. 'Well, the truck won't get through as its wheelbase is too wide, but something like a Charade probably could.'

Sandy then looked down at her feet and realised her white runners could be worse for wear after the adventure. 'I think I'll stay with the truck if that's OK. Maybe I'll go for a little wander along the riverbank track to see if I can find something.'

Nic nodded. 'Roger that.' Driver Two looked at him and shook his head.

Mrs Wilson looked at Sandy, then down at her shoes. 'I don't think my flats will make it either. I'll stay with Sandy. We could have some one-on-one girl time. I've missed out on that since Julie went AWOL.' Mrs Wilson leaned towards Sandy as they watched Driver Two and Nic head off. 'Please call me Dotty now that the men have left.'

Sandy and Dotty started to walk back along the path, and about ten minutes later, Sandy thought of a question: 'If Julie has only been missing about a day, how often did you talk?'

'Every couple of days, but mainly on the two-way radio.'

'That's an open channel network, isn't it?'

'Yes, those new-fangled mobile phone things don't work out here. No signal.' Dotty pulled her phone from the pocket of her tunic and held it up a ten-year-old Nokia. 'I don't like them anyway.' Sandy was about to respond when her phone rang. Dotty looked at her. 'That's not supposed to happen.'

Sandy sat down on a tree stump and beckoned Dotty to sit beside her. 'It's a Sat phone.... Hi Nic. What's up? You're on speaker, and Dotty is next to me.'

'Dotty?'

Sandy grinned. 'Mrs Wilson. We're on a first-name basis now.'

'Good to know. Well, we've found the car. There's nothing much else here. It's just parked, not bogged or anything. The recent rains have meant there aren't any footprints around it. I would say she or they either left the car and she or they walked back the way she or they came...or aliens have abducted them.'

Dotty chipped in. 'You keep saying she or they, and them.' Nic hesitated. 'Well, how tall was Julie?' Dotty responded. 'Under five foot. Why?'

'The driver's seat is set back. She couldn't have reached the pedals, and there's the other thing.'

'What's that?'

'A note. It reads: "Wade. Don't bother looking for her."'

9

Rose and Driver were parked outside the car museum back in Mildura, waiting for inspiration. It was closed, as Shirley had alluded to; however, there was an opportunity for them to walk the perimeter. Driver was peering through binoculars. 'The security system is state of the art. We'd have to assume the vision will be stored somewhere. I can't make out the business name, but we should be able to see it if ….' Rose responded. 'I would guess it's "Vizinary Security." They're based in Melbourne. I took a picture of the label when we were here yesterday and met a man named Hanson Fonteyn last night outside the restaurant after you went to bed. Chewy is doing a background check on them. Let's walk.'

They stepped out of the car and approached a back gate. It was locked, but Rose managed to clamber over the fence. Driver moved to stop her. 'It's still breaking and entering even if we don't enter the buildings.'

Rose nodded. 'I think that would be a fine line, given we have permission to investigate the missing car, and that's exactly what we are doing, albeit without supervision.' Rose continued moving towards the museum warehouse doors, shook on the handles, was satisfied they were secure and moved over to the work shed Ronnie had supposedly driven the car into. Rose was about to try the doors when a voice interrupted the silence: '*The Police have been notified. Stay where you are.*'

Rose looked up to the nearest camera, gave a little wave, and then headed back to the gate where Driver was waiting. 'They've called the Police.'

'I don't think so.'

'Why?'

'I've got a scanner linked to my phone. It would have beeped.'

'They could've used a mobile to call them.'

Driver shook his head. 'It doesn't work that way. This back-to-base system works via an app, and Chewy set it up on my phone just in case.'

They sat back in the car, where Rose re-read the personnel report. 'What do we do now?' Driver sighed. 'I think we should wait to see if anyone turns up.'

A late model Commodore arrived at the front gate about fifteen minutes later, and Shirley stepped out. 'You two couldn't wait, could you? I told you we're not open for a few days, and now you've interrupted my beauty sleep.'

'It's ten o'clock in the morning.'

'Anyway, now that you're here, I'll take you through.'

Shirley unlocked the gate, moved to the museum entrance, and approached the electronic keypad panel. 'It's a ten-digit sequence if you're wondering, and no, I'm not going to let you know what it is.'

The light changed to green, and she led them in. Shirley continued: 'The warehouse has about forty cars and other memorabilia, but you don't want the full tour. Follow me to the back roller door, and I'll show you what Ronnie was supposed to do.'

Driver and Rose followed her past the myriad of classic and modern motor vehicles. Rose couldn't help but stop to read about some of the cars' histories. 'This is very impressive, but why in Mildura? I thought there were rumours about a National Motor Museum being set up in Canberra.'

'Yes, and there's one at Birdwood, in the Adelaide Hills. This one is strictly for Holden badged cars.'

They reached the four-metre roller door where Shirley touched the wall button and it began to rise. 'All he did was drive it out of this shed, across the tarmac and into the work shed. Even he should have managed that without getting lost.'

Rose nodded. 'It would've taken less than a couple of seconds. We've noticed the cameras. Is there a vision of him doing that?'

'Yep, but if you don't believe me, we can review it at the office.'

Rose nodded. 'We'll do that once we're finished here. Can we get access to the work shed?' Shirley sighed. 'Yes, but I can only raise the roller door halfway. We can't go inside as the police have cordoned it off until the Detectives return from leave.' Shirley raised the door to half height, and they peered inside. The shed was empty. Driver took a step closer. 'I can still smell solvents and grease, so there must be something in there.'

Rose took a pen torch from her pocket and shone it into the space. 'Now that's interesting. If I shine my torch along the wall, it appears to bend around something, but there's nothing there. Are you sure we can't go in?'

'Nope. I have orders to let you into the museum, only to show you the work shed and the camera vision. That's it.'

'Orders from whom?'

'My bosses and the security people.'

'Who are?'

'Vizinary Security. Also, the owners are a concerned consortium of people around Mildura and beyond. If you don't like it, too bad.'

Rose nodded. 'OK, I've seen enough. Let's go to the office.'

The trio headed back through the museum and into the office where Shirley opened the computer file and clicked on the tab that contained the day of the theft. 'My computer guy arranged for our security guy to send it to me. We don't store the vision here for obvious reasons.' Rose picked up a replica model of the Commodore that had gone missing and began spinning the wheels. 'Like what?'

'Like put that down. It's worth about four hundred dollars.'

'OK. I will if you tell me what is so obvious about not storing the vision on-site.'

Shirley continued: 'For a start, the file can't be tampered with, lost, or our computer hacked, so it disappears forever.'

Driver went over to a glass wall cabinet containing other replica cars, including scale models of the Peter Brock Commodores that had won some of the famous Bathurst Car Races, then turned back to face Shirley. 'But you said they emailed you the file, and it can be intercepted and manipulated once it's on the information highway.'

'Yes, but they still have the original file in their computers.'

Driver returned to the desk. 'And if someone intercepts the file, they can reverse engineer the code and send a virus back to the originator to destroy their server.'

Shirley nodded. 'They can do that?'

'They can do anything if they know how. Please show us what else you have.'

Shirley smiled. 'You've already seen it, and there's nothing there. Both doors are open, and he drives out of one shed into another. The car comes out of one garage and into the other. Ronnie goes in and comes out. Nothing else to see here, folks.'

They watched the vision, and it was spliced into separate quadrants to show multiple images. The view was exactly as Shirley had described. It is very simple, complete, and reveals nothing. The final vision was from a camera directly pointing into the work shed, showing Ronnie stepping out of the car, shutting the car door, exiting, and then the roller door closed behind him.

Shirley pushed enter, and the vision froze. 'I told you so.'

Rose nodded. 'Is there any more?'

'Yes, it's the next bit where it gets interesting.'

Shirley hovered the mouse over the Play button and tapped it. The vision showed the roller door rising, and the car was no longer visible halfway up. The door took less than a minute to reach the top, and the car was gone. Shirley smiled. 'I hate to repeat myself, but I told you so.' Rose nodded again.

'Do you mind if we take a copy? Can you transfer the file to this thumb drive please.'

Shirley plugged the drive into the port, transferred the file, extracted it, and held it up for Rose. 'Sure, here you go, but what is the point of looking at nothing? Nothing is still nothing if nothing is there.'

'Thanks, but I'll watch it a few more times myself. I've learned that nothing can mean everything, just because it is nothing.'

'Huh?'

Rose continued. 'Just because we expect something and get nothing doesn't' necessarily mean we have nothing. It may mean everything.'

Shirley shrugged. 'That still sounds like gobble-de-gook to me.'

Both Rose and Driver smiled.

'Anything else you want to look at?'

'Nope. We'll return to our Hotel room. Thanks for your time.'

The dynamic duo went back to their car, drove off and Driver looked over to Rose as he pulled the car to a stop at their Hotel. 'You know it's got me stumped. The car went in, he went out, and it went missing. There's no rear door to get it out; if the car were moved, someone would have heard or seen it.' Rose thought about that. 'Unless the car hasn't been moved at all. I think I saw something, but I must watch the vision again. I didn't want to mention it with Shirley in the room.' Driver sighed. 'What did you see?'

'It's more what I didn't see that doesn't make sense.'

'Please don't do that. You've been working with Nic too long and are starting to sound like him.'

Rose booted up her computer a few minutes later, uploaded the drive and ran the vision. The installed software allowed it to be slowed down to frame by frame.

Driver was watching intensely. 'What exactly are you looking for?'

'Wait...it's when the roller door goes up after Ronnie has moved out.... There.'

Rose froze the screen. 'Watch the left corner. There's a bat or a small bird. It could be a sparrow.'

Rose pressed play.

Driver continued to watch but saw nothing. 'What am I looking at?'

'The bird disappears.'

10

Back in Murrayville, Nic, Sandy, and Driver Two were at Dotty's place enjoying a cup of tea and hummingbird cake despite her determined intentions to serve them more coffee with it. 'Are you sure you want to stick with tea?' They all nodded in agreement. Nic unfurled the map on the kitchen table and ran his finger along the line of Dawson's Creek. 'What's on the other side of the river here?'

'Dobbie Dunstan lives there. He's a bit of a loner and keeps that sort of thing to himself. He might know if any canoes have been used recently. I can call him up on the two-way radio if you like.'

Nic nodded. 'Yep, please. He might have seen something.' Dotty lifted the handset of the two-way radio from the cradle. 'Dotty...calling Dobbie, are you on channel? Dotty calling Dobbie. Are you on channel Dobbie?'

They waited, but there wasn't a response.

Driver Two looked up. 'He might not have it turned on. Can we try his phone?'

'He doesn't do technology apart from the two-way; we must always keep them on. It's part of our Community Watch stuff. We have to look out for each other. Fire and flood emergency, alien abductions. That sort of thing.' A woman's voice responded instead. 'Dotty. This is Nicole. Dobbie's taken a few days off. He told me about having to meet someone somewhere to do something for somebody.'

Sandy blurted out. 'Hey, are you Nicole, as in Nic Thorn's sister?'

Dotty looked at her. 'It could've been, but I didn't have the handset switched on, so she wouldn't have heard you. Did you want to try again?' Nic smiled. 'That wasn't my sister, and there are at least five other Nic's that live around the Murrayville area. Let alone those who are on channel. It's a very popular name you know: Nic Kidman, Nic Nolte, Saint Nic and Nic-myself-while-shaving.'

Sandy muttered. 'Damn you, Nic.' The woman's voice responded. 'I'm sorry, who said that? Do you have other people with you, Dotty?'

'Yes indeed. I've got Nic Thorn, Sandy Fraser and Driver Two. They're looking into the disappearance of Julie Wilson.'

'OK. Hi Nic, your sister wants to know if you're still attending the Ouyen Primary School reunion.

It's finally on tonight after two years of delay due to COVID.'

Nic responded. 'Please tell Nic I'm in the middle of this thing and can't spare the time.' Driver Two and Sandy shook their heads disappointedly, and Nic continued: 'Besides, we're heading to Canberra once this mystery is sorted.'

The caller continued: 'Come on, Nic, you haven't seen her since you were last here, and that was when you were looking into that bottle recycling scam that Wade was running across to the South Australian border.'

'OK. I'll think about it then.' Nic lowered the handset, took his finger from the talk button, and clicked it back on. 'Thought about it, and nope, I'm not coming.'

A cacophony of voices came through the speaker as if everyone wanted to note their disappointment simultaneously. Then the gaggle of chatter morphed into a garbled mess until someone told everyone else to get off the call.

Finally a man's voice finally commandeered the conversation: 'Can everyone stop talking, please? I suppose it's important; he's here to find my wife, so I had him come down from Brisbane to look for her.' Nic responded. 'Good call out, Wade. I didn't realise you were on channel.'

'Everyone's on channel Nic, but we usually tune out. Anyway, did you find her?'

Nic clicked the microphone button. 'I think we'd better take this offline, Wade.'

'OK. Come to my place this arvo then. I'm having a rehearsal with a couple of mates. We're putting on a little performance for the school reunion and thought you might like to see what we have been working on.'

Nic smiled. 'Roger that.'

Driver Two shook his head. 'Please stop with the 'Roger That.'

Nic looked at him and nodded. 'Roger Will-Co. We'll see you this arvo.' Nic then placed the handset back in the cradle. 'OK, at least we've got the rest of the morning to find Julie. I think we'll start by going back to Dobbie Dunstan's place. Can we borrow the truck? We'll bring Julie's car back with us.'

Dotty nodded. 'Then what?'

Nic smiled. 'Then we watch a jam session at Wade's place.'

Driver Two, Nic and Sandy returned to Dawson's Creek; recovered the car and loaded it onto the tray. The tray mechanism lifted and slid back until it was flat on the ground, so all they had to do was roll the car onto it.

Sandy had ventured further up the riverbank and then returned. 'Nic, I think they didn't use a canoe, but there's something I want you to look at. We'll have to go down onto the riverbank as you can't see it from the track.' Sandy led them forward and relocated the area. 'It's one of those ex-army floating bridges. It looks like it's been rolled up.'

'Good find. I'll go to the other side and see what this is.' Nic stepped into the water and took a deep breath. 'Cripes, it's cold.' Driver Two decided to follow him into the water. 'But the river is not deep, so why use it here?'

They reached the other side and folded out the bridge. It spanned across the creek, so they set it in place and secured the tie ropes to test the strength, and it quickly took their weight. Driver Two wiped the mud from his hands. 'I don't think this was an alien abduction as they wouldn't have to use a bridge. They can teleport, you know. I've seen it on the internet.'

Nic nodded. 'You know, I didn't know that. Anyway, I would say we've worked out what happened to Julie. She's found a new friend in Dobbie Dunstan and has most likely taken off with him.'

Nic folded out the note found in the car and re-read it. 'I would say Dobbie has had something to do with her going missing as they most kindly left this note, and it's got his name and address on the back. I wish solving cases of missing people was always this easy.' Sandy nodded. 'But perhaps it might not be that easy. It might be she's left

Wade for greener pastures, and Dobbie helped her escape, or she's gone on a holiday without him.'

'Yep, to all that. Let's return to Murrayville and drop the car off at Wade's. I'll jam with him and drop the truck back at Dotty's. If we're not too exhausted, we'll attend the reunion.'

Driver Two looked at him. 'You're still planning on going?'

'Yep. Always was, always will be.'

'And you want us to come too?'

'Yep. I'm going dressed as The Batman, Sandy will be Robin, and you'll be Alfred, my Butler.'

'Won't they recognise you?'

'I don't think so. Gotham City is a lot bigger than Ouyen, and no one notices that Bruce Wayne is The Batman in that mega-metropolis.'

Driver Two nodded. 'OK...but don't you think I'm a little too large to be Alfred? Besides, he doesn't wear a disguise.' Nic nodded. 'Good point. We might have to wing it. You've already met Dotty and Wade, so our disguises might just fool the others.'

The trio drove to Wade's place and unloaded Julie's car. Wade was busying himself with three others rehearsing, so he hadn't noticed they'd arrived and eventually found him in the machinery shed. One musician was banging away on a makeshift set of drums. It comprised two forty-four-gallon ex-petrol containers and was alternating between the two. Wade was playing an electric guitar through a pair of speakers about two metres high, and another man was playing a bass guitar. They didn't stop playing despite attempts to get their attention.

Nic flicked off the mains power switch however the drummer kept drumming as he had his eyes closed. 'Why did we stop?' He looked at them. 'Because Wade asked me to find his wife, and I'm here to tell him what's happened to her.'

Wade looked at him. 'I thought you were here to help us with these songs.'

Sandy shook her head. 'Don't you want to know where she is?'

'Not really. She'll probably come back when she gets hungry or bored.'

Sandy added. 'We think she's run off with Dobbie Dunstan.'

'How do you know that? Did he leave a note?'

Nic unfurled the piece of paper and handed it to him. 'Yep.'

'Wow. I thought she might have. I've wondered why she was spending so much time next door. She told me to give myself some space to play my music. I even asked him to join the band, too. Never mind.' Wade started strumming again and Sandy shook her head. 'Don't you want to find her?'

'Not really. She's probably next door and might even be at the reunion tonight I'll chat with other people to see when or if she's returning. She would be missing her cows.' Nic looked at him. 'So, you asked me to come from Brisbane on the pretence that Julie was missing, yet you knew all along she might be at the reunion?' Wade shrugged. 'How else was I going to get you there? Besides, I bet it's been a while since you've had some real fun.' Sandy and Driver Two looked at Nic to see how he would react, but it wasn't what they expected. 'Firstly, we must work something out. Which guitar do you want me to play?'

11

In Mildura, Rose and Driver were waiting outside the perimeter gates of the museum. They'd asked all the staff to meet them to reveal that they'd recovered the car. Rose had just been on the phone with Chewy, and he'd confirmed her suspicions regarding the mystery. A couple of cars arrived that held Shirley, Ronnie, the Mayor, and her bodyguard, and then Barrie pulled up in a Police Car with the constable. Rose nodded. 'We're still waiting on Hanson Fonteyn.'

Barrie moved over to Driver. 'Do you think he'll give us any trouble?'

Shirley overheard. 'Who? Hanson Fonteyn? He's as gentle as a lamb.'

Barrie then folded out a piece of paper so Shirley could read it. It was an arrest warrant for Hanson Fonteyn, who also used an alias: Felix Knight.

'You didn't tell me you were here to arrest him the other day?'

'He wasn't here.'

'What makes you think he'll be here now, then?'

Rose stepped in. 'Because he thinks he's too clever to get caught.'

They didn't have to wait long as another car arrived. It was a late-model Rolls Royce Silver Shadow convertible. Hanson Fonteyn pulled the vehicle to a stop and climbed out. 'Sorry I'm late; I've been busy organising a buyer for this car.' Driver moved forward and firmly shook his hand. 'Thank you for coming.'

Rose nodded to Shirley, but the others didn't know what was happening. 'We're not going through the museum, just to the work shed.'

The group played Follow the Leader and stood by the high roller door a few minutes later. It was half open, and again, the building appeared empty.

Ronnie shook his head. 'So where's the car? I thought you said you'd found it.'

Rose nodded towards the space. 'I have. It's in there.'

Driver and Barrie quietly stepped behind Fonteyn to close down any escape attempt; however, as Hanson didn't notice, he crossed his arms over his chest and smiled: 'You brought us here to show us nothing? I'm leaving.'

Barrie clamped a hand down on his shoulder. 'We'd like you to stay around a little longer, son.'

Rose then extracted a torch from her bag and shone it into the space. 'Watch the beam.' The group leaned forward and Rose continued: 'There.' Shirley took another step forward. 'What are we looking for?'

'That's the point. There's nothing in there, apparently.'

Rose then shone the torch onto the nearest camera. It showed a security system labelled 'Vizinary Security'. 'How long has the security system been in place?'

Shirley responded. 'About two months. We needed to upgrade it as we'd heard a rumour that some of our cars were being ...um...made available for sale, but no one here knew anything about it.' Rose continued: 'So, you installed the system, and an expensive Commodore has gone missing two months later. Didn't you find that a little suspicious?' Driver watched for Hanson's reaction, and then Rose added. 'And Mr Fonteyn wouldn't know anything about that, would he?'

Fonteyn took a step backward and ran into Barrie, who folded out his arrest warrant and handed it to him. 'This is for you. Welcome back to Mildura.'

Shirley looked at Barrie. 'He'd told me he'd never been here before.'

'Well, he hadn't as Hanson Fonteyn, but under the guise of a security systems installer named Felix Knight, he and his team from Vizinary Security spent time setting this up.'

Ronnie stepped forward to be beside his mother. 'I still don't see the car.'

Rose looked at him. 'Be my guest and go inside. Move slowly, though, as you might injure yourself in the car. You can't see it, but it's definitely there.'

Ronnie moved into the vacant space, and the others watched for a reaction. As he stepped further inside, a sparrow flew from a nest on the left-hand side of the shed, then suddenly disappeared only to appear a couple of seconds later, gliding towards the right-hand side wall. It then flew out the open roller door. Everyone except Fonteyn watched it in flight as he knew what would happen.

Ronnie took another step forward and sensed himself falling into space. 'There's something here. It's a screen, like a plastic curtain.' He turned towards the others, faced the screen again, and carefully put his hands forward into the space. 'I can feel something solid.' Then, the lad looked down at his feet and noticed the tips of his shoes were missing. 'Wow. This is amazing.' He pushed at the 'wall' before him, and it rippled. 'They've hidden the car behind a movie screen and projected a view of the empty shed onto the screen.' Ronnie kicked his foot forward, and it clunked against something solid. 'I've found the car.'

He leaned towards his feet, found the bottom of the screen, and started to tug at it. Fonteyn called out. 'Don't do that, Ronnie. Tell him to stop. The screens are worth about eighty thousand dollars each, and the cameras might get damaged. They're worth about three thousand bucks a pop.'

Barrie nodded. 'Come out now, Ronnie. We've got this from here.' Fonteyn turned to Rose. 'One more day, that's all we needed. We almost got it out. How did you know?'

Rose smiled. 'The bird. It disappeared from vision on the screen. I knew it had to be an illusion or a trick, and I knew the car couldn't have been moved without someone noticing, so I searched how an illusionist makes elephants and buildings disappear. They do it with mirrors, but in your case, it's a lot more high-tech and involves several cameras and a couple of large flexible Perspex screens.'

Barrie placed handcuffs onto his wrists and handed him over to the Constable.

A couple of hours later, Rose, Driver, Barrie, Ronnie, and Shirley were at the Mildura Brewery Pub celebrating the recovery of the 'lost' Commodore. Barrie placed the next round on the table and held up his glass: 'Thanks to Nic Thorn and Associates for finding something that wasn't lost. Oh, and for getting Hanson Fonteyn, aka Felix Knight, to accept my warrant for his arrest gracefully. We'd been chasing him and his company around Victoria for about two years, and we'd just received a call about a warehouse held by Vizinary Security that contains several cars, a couple of high-end boats and even a fifth-wheeler caravan. They had an elaborate set-up, undercutting any existing security company arrangement and then waiting a few months to start their 'missing' vehicle capers. They've left many confused and angry people in their wake, so if your guys are available, we'd be happy for you to join us at the Mornington Peninsula to help us recover the rest of their 'stolen' merchandise.'

Rose held up her glass to acknowledge the offer. 'Thanks, but no thanks. We only investigate, infiltrate, and obfuscate.' Driver stood up. 'Rose found the connection between Vizinary Security and increased thefts just after they installed their security operations. It all came together from there, but we must move on as we're have to go to Murrayville to investigate a missing person.'

A woman's voice interrupted the banter. 'Do you need my help? There's no longer a budget for a bodyguard in the Mildura council, so I'm looking for a career change. I can appear a little overbearing at times. Who knew?'

Barrie looked her up and down. 'Do you know how to serve a warrant? Shirley and I would like to retire and do the ski-ing stuff.'

The large woman nodded. 'I can learn.'

Ronnie took a sip of his beer. 'But you guys don't like the snow.' Shirley put her hand on his forearm. 'Nope, but we'll enjoy Spending the Kid's Inheritance.'

12

Meanwhile, in Murrayville, Nic struggled to make himself more comfortable as he was dressed a figure-hugging Batman suit, and Driver Two was dressed as his butler, Alfred. 'I can't see how this will work, Nic, as soon as you arrive, they'll know it's you disguised as The Batman.' Nic started to respond, but it came out a little garbled, so he felt for the join in his mask from under his chin, then rolled it downwards to speak more clearly. 'You're probably right, but Bruce Wayne has got away with it since 1939. I'm sure I'll be fine. Damn, I should've thought this through. I can't sing much if I can't move my mouth because of the latex covering my jaw.' He raised the mask, worked his jaw, and tried to speak. It didn't work.

A moment later, Sandy came up to join them. 'Hey, my name is not spelled correctly' then she pulled at the name badge on the uniform. 'It should be Robin with an I not Robyn with a why.' Nic nodded, then lowered his mask. 'But you're a lady Robin, so it's spelled correctly. I googled it. Some men use the name spelled Robyn. It's one of those ambidextrous names.'

'Don't you mean androgynous?'

'I've no idea. Let me google that, too. Damn, no network.' Nic raised the mask again to cover his mouth, and the terrific trio climbed into their hire car for the hundred-kilometre trip to Ouyen.

Nic looked at his phone and tried to speak; again, it came out garbled, so he lowered the latex...again. 'This is getting tedious. How do the masked Avengers manage? I've just Googled "Ouyen" for your info. The population is around one thousand, the town is around a hundred years old, and people come from around the world yearly to celebrate past and present residents, then there's the big dead tree that keeps everyone stumped.'

Sandy called out from the back seat. 'I can't see how this will work; as soon as you arrive, they'll know it's you disguised as The Batman.'

'I must have powers of Deja-vu. I've already heard that before somewhere.'

Driver shook his head. 'You're nervous, aren't you? I haven't seen you like this for a while. You usually say things profound and sprout gobble-de-gook, but it's like you've forgotten who you are.'

'No, I haven't. I'm The Batman.'

They reached the Ouyen town sign about an hour later, and Driver slowed the car down. 'OK, where are we headed?' Nic mumbled. 'It's just off ...um. I guess you look for the Old Courthouse. It's opposite the IGA.' Nic nodded towards the 'Ouyen Primary School Reunion' sign. 'Most likely, that'll work too. I haven't been here since...a while anyway.'

Driver followed the signs and found a park near a Bat-mobile parked at the curb in front of a large marquee. The car replicates the 1955 Lincoln Future from the 1960s Batman series. 'I suspect this is the place, my dynamic duo.'

They stepped from their car and headed towards the tent, where a host acknowledged them and held back the tent flap for them to enter: 'Welcome, Batman, nineteen, Robin, sixteen and Alfred, twelve. Please join the others.' Sandy and Driver entered, and it was wall-to-wall superheroes, well, at least two or three, if you included Alfred as a superhero by association. Nic hesitated a little and waited for another group of partygoers to enter. 'I'm The Batman. Welcome to The Bat Cave.'

A portly gentleman was dressed in the same latex 'Batman' suit; however, it was most unflattering. His mask was pulled down over his chin so he could talk more easily. 'I'm The Batman too. This is my wife, Robyn, and our butler, Fred.'

Nic shook their hands. 'I think you mean Alfred and your side-kick Robin.'

The man shrugged, and the man dressed as Alfred looked at Nic and held out his hand. 'I'm Al Williams. I live over in Lameroo… I went to the Primary school in the late seventies and can't remember any Batman in the class. We had a few jokers, but not any one called Batman Anyway, who are you under that disguise?'

Nic smiled. 'Call me Bruce, Bruce Wayne.'

The man shrugged again. 'You know there were a couple of Wayne's at the school, and of course a few Bruce's. When did you go to school here?'

Nic responded. 'I can't remember…it's too long ago.' Nic then held the tent flap open for them to move inside, and he headed off to find Sandy and Driver Two, which was a challenge as around sixty people were dressed the same. He finally found Sandy talking to Wade. 'Whose idea was it to dress as caped crusaders?'

Wade took a swig of his beer. 'You'll have to ask Nic, as he organised all the costumes. Have you seen him? We're due to give our performance in five minutes.' Nic tapped him on the shoulder. 'I'm here. I saw the bat signal.'

Sandy shook her head. 'So how are you going to play in front of everyone? What about privacy, protection, and all the other Batman stuff?' Nic nodded. 'You know I haven't worked how yet. Besides that, how am I going to be able to sing without taking my mask off.'

Meantime, the other band members had walked up: 'Ready, guys? Let's get up there....' Two men dressed as Batman moved over to the stage, waiting for the Emcee to make the introduction, and Sandy noticed Nic had moved around to the other side of the stage and then disappeared behind the stage curtain. The two stepped onto the stage from the front while the drummer and Nic entered behind the curtain. They readied themselves and waited for the Emcee to introduce them:

'Ladies and Gentlemen, or Batmen, Alfred's, and Robins. Welcome to the Ouyen Primary School reunion. Please let me introduce you to Gotham City's finest, who will open our show with their rendition of the Batman theme, then do a couple of other batty songs.'

The band started with the Batman theme, then played 'Bat (Bad) Man (Moon) Rising, House of the Rising Bat (Sun) and a funky version of Bat out of Hell by Meatloaf. The band managed to keep in time and finished together. It was quite an achievement, given their apparent lack of rehearsals.

They bowed, then waited for the Emcee to introduce them formally: 'We have Wade Wilson on rhythm guitar.' Wade removed his face mask and nodded to the crowd. 'His brother Karl on drums.' Karl stood up from behind the drums and waived.

'Their other brother Woody on lead guitar.' Woody jumped down and did a few air guitar moves for the crowd, aka Elvis Presley, with arm-swinging circles.

Sandy took a breath as she knew Nic was next. 'And...um...a Batman on lead.'

The Batman waived, then exited without raising his mask. The audience watched him leave, and someone called out: 'Who was that masked man?'

Sandy took the opportunity to follow him and met him at the back of the stage. 'That was close. I thought you were going to have to show your face.' The Batman nodded, so Sandy leaned up and kissed him lightly on his exposed cheek. 'And good job on the borrowed guitar, by the way.'

Driver Two saw them together and ambled up. 'You did a good job. It was a good show.' The Batman nodded again, then leaned towards Sandy, looking for another congratulatory kiss. Sandy obliged, hugged, and headed out of the backstage area, where he bent forward, waiting for another kiss.

Sandy stepped back. 'Since when do you show public affection, Nic?' The Batman stopped and removed his mask. 'Who is Nic? I'm Wayne.' Driver Two and Sandy looked at him. 'Wayne, who?'

'Wayne Bruse. I played the lead guitar. My Father was a Wayne Bruse, too. He was the Headmaster at the Primary school. I assumed that's why the reunion was a Batman and Robin show. Whenever my name was read out at a school assembly, they called it out backward as they do....Bruse, Wayne...and of course, it would raise a chorus of 'na,na,na,na Batman'. Kids can be so cruel at school.' Wayne bowed, then moved off to join his own Robin and Alfred.

A few hours later, the party was winding up and another couple entered the tent. They weren't in disguise. The man was in a wheelchair with his left leg in plaster up to his thigh. Wade quickly moved up to them, punched the man in the chest and the man rocked back. 'Nice to see you again, Wade. No harm done. Julie and I have just come to say our goodbyes.' Julie turned the wheelchair around, and the couple left.

Sandy came up to Wade. 'Aren't you going to go after them?'

'Nope. Good riddance to them. I've got better things to do, like saving this city from nasty criminals.' Wade pulled his cape around him, ran to the Bat-mobile, jumped in and drove off. Driver watched him go. 'The original Bat-mobile from the '60s show recently sold in America for more than four million dollars?'

'Would that one be worth that much?'

'Not sure, but it could explain what Wade has been doing with all his money instead of keeping Julie happy. Happy wife, happy life, and all that.'

Sandy turned, and they went back into the tent. 'Hey, have you seen Nic? It's getting late, and we should return to Murrayville.'

'Last time I saw him, he talked to his sister.'

'Where...Who?... What does she look like?'

Driver shrugged. 'Not sure as she's dressed as a Robin.'

Sandy tried to pick a Batman talking to a Robin, but dozens of them still existed and Driver noticed Sandy was a little discouraged. 'Here comes Nic, The Batman.' Nic ambled up. 'Riddle me this, Robin. When is the best time to take your leave? No idea? When you're a tree.'

Sandy punched him. 'K-pow Batman. Let's go.'

The tenacious trio went back to the car and climbed in. Driver started the engine, and they had to wait for a flock of departing Robins to move out of the way before driving off. Sandy called from the rear seat: 'It must've been good to catch up with your sister again, but how did you find her as she was in disguise?'

Nic shrugged, stepped out of the car, removed the latex suit and mask, and dropped it on the seat behind him. He had a T-shirt and light jeans underneath. Sandy had watched the strip show. 'I didn't think anything was worn under the Batman suit.' Nic shrugged again. 'No, that's a kilt, not a Batman costume.' He then put on a northern English accent: 'Nothing is worn under a Scotsman's kilt either, as everything is in perfect working order.'

Sandy shook her head. 'Now, Sean would have made a great Batman and was by far the best James Bond. My second vote for the best Batman goes to Val Kilmer.'

Nic continued with his usual tone: 'We're catching up with Driver Two and Rose tomorrow morning for breakfast in Murrayville, and then we're heading off to our next investigation. We've been called to look into a major equipment leasing fraud. The life of a crime fighter never wains, Bruce.' Sandy picked up the mask and slapped him on his head. 'Stop with the Batman stuff. It's driving us batty.'

In the morning, Driver and Rose waited at the Cobb & Co. Café in Murrayville for the others to join them. Driver was on his second helping of scrambled eggs and couldn't get enough of the coffee being served. The waitress came back the third time with the coffee pot. 'It's a local brew. I'll let Dotty know you like it. Maybe you can take a packet or two for the road.'

Driver nodded. 'Sure. I'll take three packets.'

His brothers, Nic and Sandy, arrived and sat in the booth to order their breakfast. Driver took another swig from the coffee mug. 'Have you guys tried the coffee yet? It tastes like the stuff I used to grind myself.'

Driver Two nodded. 'We know.'

Sandy and Rose were sitting opposite each other. 'So, how was the reunion?'

Sandy gave a little cheer. 'I almost met Nic's twin sister.'

Nic smiled. 'Yep, and apparently, I did such a good job playing Batman that no one saw through my disguise. Anyway, Chewy has sent me the updated brief of this equipment leasing scandal. A group of Bankers have been defrauded, and you can bank on them not being happy.'

Rose shook her head and looked at him. 'We already know about it, as he mentioned it months ago. We are off to Canberra. It's about an eight-hour drive.'

Nic nodded. 'Unless we fly.'

Driver Two looked at him. 'How about you three fly in one of those little Cessna things and let Rose and I drive?'

'Nope, but how about we all drive back to Melbourne, then you and your brother head down to Geelong to catch up with your Mother for her eightieth birthday and let Sandy, Rose and I fly business class to Canberra.' Rose considered the response. 'So, the Drivers aren't collaborating with us on this one?'

'Nope. We have another driver who will be meeting us in Canberra.'

'What's his name?... And don't tell me it's Driver Three.'

'Nope. It's her. Polly. She's a Canberran local. There are so many pollies in Canberra, so we'll have to ensure we get the right one.'

Nic, Sandy, and Rose said their goodbyes to the two Drivers and waited for their plane to taxi to the runway for the flight to Canberra. They were seated together, and Nic was in the adjacent seat. Sandy noticed Nic had his eyes closed, so she leaned towards Rose. 'I was talking to one of the Alfreds at the reunion, and he told me Nic's Father used to be one of the magistrates at the Ouyen Courthouse, so I went for a little wander through the building but couldn't find any 'Thorn' listed on the honour board.'

'And?' Sandy sighed. 'Well, don't you think that's odd?'

'Not really...it could be that they stopped using the board or ....' Nic opened one

eye. 'Or that his surname wasn't Thorn, or maybe my name isn't Nic Thorn .'

13

The flight to Canberra was relatively uneventful; however, Sandy was intrigued by Nic's statement regarding his father's surname and continued to badger him:

'Come on, just a slither...a wafer...at least a nibble...' They were waiting at the luggage carousel when Nic finally succumbed: 'OK, seeing that I can't get you to drop your undeniable quest to know everything about me and my past, I'll let you in on some of my family secrets.'

Sandy smiled, and Rose shook her head. 'We don't need to know, and you know we don't need to know. You know.'

'I think you do.'

They waited, and he kept them waiting when Sandy finally had had enough. 'Are you going to tell us something then?'

'About what?'

Sandy softly punched him in the shoulder, then leaned down to collect her suitcase. 'We want to know some of the deep, dark secrets of the Thorns dynasty.'

'Sure, but not here or today, as this place can't keep any secrets.' Nic then moved away to chase his suitcase before it went back behind the mysterious black plastic flaps to join the cache of unclaimed luggage.

Rose moved closer to Sandy. 'In Canberra, everything is kept a secret until it needs to be known. It's the town of secrets. It's so secret they even founded the Australian Freemasons here.'

Sandy nodded. 'Really?' Rose continued. 'We could shake on it, but I don't know which secret squirrel handshake we should use. We need to find a Freemason, and they still meet secretly.' Sandy opened her phone and was searching Google to confirm the Freemason's history when an elfin-faced young woman approached them. 'Hi, I'm Polly, and I will be your Driver.'

They shook hands, and she continued. 'Nic asked me to collect you here.'

Sandy looked around for Nic and wondered whether he'd gone beyond the black sleeves in his haste to chase his luggage. Polly corralled their luggage. 'I haven't been given many details about where or what I'm supposed to do with you, but if you follow me to the carpark, I'll deliver you to the apartment.'

Sandy noticed the luggage carousel was now empty. 'Where's Nic gone? Is he joining us, or did he go behind the plastic flaps and never be seen again?'

Polly shrugged. 'He's gone off to meet up with his father. He's an elusive character that, much like his son. I haven't been formally introduced to him, and it's quite a covert operation when I drive him around the city. My instructions are always to remain seated in the car, and the privacy shield must always be closed. I think he has something to do with the American Secret Service or ASIO, but I'm not sure.'

Rose nodded. 'Interesting.'

Polly led them to a black Holden Statesman and turned around to continue her conversation. 'Oh no, it's not interesting at all. It's quite boring, and only a few times have I needed to take counter-measures to ensure his safety. I even had to drive along the bike path around Lake Burley Griffin as he suspected he was once being followed. It turned out they were part of his entourage.'

Polly's phone buzzed, so she took the call, and her demeanor changed once she had disconnected. 'That was Nic. He says I'm talking too much.'

Sandy smiled. 'Do you know what his Father's name is?'

'I think it's Thorn, but I don't know his first name. I haven't got that far as yet.'

Rose nodded. 'How long have you been driving for him?'

'Since I left school.'

Sandy and Rose looked at her. 'So how old are you then? Twenty?'

'No...but thanks. I'm thirty next month. Nic told me you guys are about the same age, but I've picked you as much older....'

Polly's phone rang again; she took the call, then disconnected. 'That was Nic again. I'm not supposed to ask about your ages, either. I've been driving in Canberra for about five years, and before that, I was in the Service....as an Ambulance Driver. Feel free to call me 'Ambo' if you like. Polly is just my pseudonym.'

Rose leaned forward. 'OK, then, Polly. Do you know if this car is bugged?'

'I don't think so, as that might be an invasion of privacy, but I know that the Thorns like to keep secrets.' Rose sat back. 'So how come Nic knows what you're saying then?' Polly shrugged. 'I've always assumed my phone is bugged. Anyhow, we're here.' They stopped outside the Canberra Cemetery. Polly climbed out and moved towards the gatehouse.

Sandy pressed the button to lower her window. 'I don't think this is anything like a five-star hotel. I was expecting so much more from Canberra.'

Rose smiled. 'At least the neighbours won't trouble us, and we're in the dead centre of town.'

Polly returned a few minutes later with a huge dark brown dog and opened the passenger door. The dog obediently climbed in, Polly clipped the seatbelt around him and he sat there waiting for Polly to go around to the driver's side. 'This is 'Cadbury'. He's part German wirehaired pointer and part Chocolate Labrador.'

Sandy nodded, leaned forward, and patted the brown dog on the head. 'I've always wanted a chocolate pointer as they're so convenient at Easter time. Rose and I adopted one of Australia's largest cat breeds; he's a pure breed Maine Coon. We call him "Dog"'.

Polly came around to the driver's side and climbed in. 'Nic told me about him and that your cat has even solved a mystery.' Polly pulled at the tuft of hair under the dog's chin. 'All this one does is point out chocolate. He's just like a chocolate milkshake, only doggy.' Sandy nodded. 'Our Dog is a fully-fledged superhero. We investigated a banking scam, and it turned out that the guy's Father owned our cat before we did. His name was Matt.'

'The cat's name was Matt?'

'No, the banker. We unmasked the loan arranger as a fraud. He...oh, never mind. Is this where we're staying?' Polly smiled. 'No. You're at the Pacifica Apartments on Northbourne. It's just down from the London Circuit. Close to all the action but far enough away from all the noise from the house on the hill.'

'Which house?'

'Parliament House.'

Polly started the engine, and the dog dropped its left paw onto the electric window button; the window lowered, and the dog put his enormous head out: 'Woof.'

Sandy lowered hers and put her head out, too. 'I agree, Cadbury. Woof.'

They drove off, and Polly stopped outside the Lynham Animal Rescue Centre.

'Sorry, did I mention I'm a vet?'

Rose responded. 'Nope, but you did say you were in the Service.'

'Sorry, I'm a real ...hang on...I'm a veterinarian. Not a vet, vet. I'm rostered on at the moment. I do locum work. The guys running this clinic are short-staffed due to the ...breeding season, so I have to take a quick visit to ensure everything is OK. I won't be long. Cadbury will keep you company.' Polly tossed the car fob onto the passenger seat. 'Cadbury is not allowed to drive but listens to talk-back radio. I leave him with the keys in case he gets bored and wants to change the channel.'

Rose and Sandy were waiting for Polly to return when Nic approached the car; he sat in the driver's seat and commandeered the key fob to turn the radio off. 'Polly has been detained as one of the politicians' cats is giving birth to quintuplets, so I'll be your driver. You can call me ...um...Driver Nic.'

Rose smiled. 'How did your soiree go with your father?'

'He's still the same. He doesn't say much and plays his cards close to his chest. Likes to keep secrets, that sort of thing.'

'Like father, like son.'

'Oh no. I haven't had any secrets anymore since I met you two. Shall we go?'

'Sure, Driver Nic, but can I ask you a personal question?'

'Sure, Passenger Rose, as long as it's not about my father.'

'Does your Mother know what your Father does?'

'Very funny, but I will tell you this. He's come away from the Murrayville farm to be here today.' Rose thought about the comment and then realised what the implication meant. 'So, he runs the family farm as a tax minimisation scheme?'

Nic nodded. 'Exactly, and it's all legal. After all, we're in the Family Trust and tax minimisation capital of the world here in Canberra. They even publish a book about it every couple of years, then a nice man gives a speech about it.'

'You mean The Budget and the Treasurer compiles it. It's a called a release, not a publication, and it's not for bedside reading.'

'Damn, I was hoping it would replace my Gideons Bible.'

They drove down Northbourne Avenue, and Nic pulled the car into the driveway of the hotel complex and then went inside to complete the booking. The young receptionist looked up at Nic and then over to Rose and Sandy: 'It shows a booking for three apartments for three weeks. Which one of you is Ms Thorn?'

Nic smiled. 'They both are. This is Rose Thorn, and this is Sandy Thorn. They are the thorns in my side.' The receptionist went to respond but thought better of it. The group returned to the car, drove into the underground carpark, ascended the elevator, and located rooms.

Rose and Sandy dropped their luggage off and went directly to Nic's room, where the coffee percolator was already perking. Sandy slumped down in the nearest chair. 'So, are we really your sisters on this one?'

'Actually, we might not need names, but we'll likely need more helpers. Our brief is not very brief either; it's a complete dossier.'

Nic handed each of them a folder containing around twenty pages of information, including background notes on each person implicated in the investigation. It also included five pages of inventory. 'We're calling it The Little Lyneham Leasing Scam.'

Rose joined Sandy and sat down to read their files. Rose was the first to finish and look up. 'Good name, and how original. From what I've read, it looks like two banks here in Lyneham were competing for the same opportunity when one got the jump on the other by under-cutting the interest rate, but now they've both lost out.'

'Yep. After settling the refinancing deal, the incoming banker looked into the corporation and realised the whole thing was a scam. The first bank people should have completed a site visit or at least sighted photographic evidence of the equipment. They did neither. I'm not sure why.'

Rose leafed through the pages and found the one she was looking for. 'And that's why we've been brought in to investigate. It shows here that most of the equipment was being stored in shipping containers at an address in Queanbeyan. Has someone been out there to check it out?

'That would be us.'

'What are we expecting to find if the equipment has already been moved on and out?' Nic smiled. 'Empty shipping containers.'

Sandy shook her head. 'So, we've come all this way to look at nothing?'

Nic continued, 'Not quite. Finding nothing would be the start, and then we work backward from the emptiness. Sort of like staring into a black hole of government spending.' Rose continued. 'OK. I have another question. When do we leave, as we both need to change into our super-sleuth uniforms?' Nic nodded. 'I think mine is at the dry cleaners. Anyway, Polly has just texted me to say another locum can take over for the duration of the investigation and will meet us here within the hour.'

'OK, Question three. When do we get to meet your father?'

'He'll be around somewhere. Canberra has lots of round-a-bouts.' Rose put down her coffee. 'Polly drives him around but hasn't formally been introduced to him as yet. Why is that?'

'You know the drill, privacy stuff and all that. Besides, I don't even know where he lives. For all I know, he might live in the big round thing on the hill.'

Sandy smiled. 'So, he is a politician.'

Nic shrugged. 'I'm not sure what he does. He could be working in the radio tower atop Black Mountain.' Nic was about to continue when his phone chimed. 'Polly's back already, so I'll bring her up. Just message me when you guys are done putting on your disguises.'

Rose and Sandy left the room, and Polly came in with Cadbury moments later. 'I caught the tram with Cadbury. I told them he was a sniffer dog on duty, but he only ever finds the half-eaten Mars Bars.'

Nic nodded. 'I expect nothing less from half-breed Chocolate Pointer.'

14

About forty minutes later, the group were heading to Queanbeyan, about a twenty-minute drive north of Canberra. They drove through the town, and Polly turned right into Captains Flat Road as she needed to stop to inspect some llamas. As they climbed out of the car, Cadbury sat in the front seat waiting for further instructions. Sandy held the door open for the him. 'Doesn't Cadbury want to come with us?' Polly shrugged. 'No, he gets quite anxious around the llamas. Last week, we watched Dr Doolittle, not the recent Hollywood one, the other one with Rex Harrison, and when he led the 'Push-Me-Pull-You' out of the crate, Cadbury hid behind the couch.'

The group moved to the pens and found an elderly couple waiting for Polly. 'Hi Polly, thanks for coming. Something has got the llamas spooked. It might just be the alpacas that have moved in next door.'

Nic looked at the beasts. 'Do you mean the llamas are alarmed? That's alarming.'

The elderly woman looked at him. 'I'm sorry, was that supposed to be funny?'

'Not really. I was checking.'

The woman looked at Nic. 'Can you stand over there, please? Beware the llama's spit.' The woman pointed towards the pen where two male llamas were. Nic nodded and quietly moved to stand by the rail. He was about to say something else when one of the male llamas spat at him, and the glob landed on his shoulder.

Polly entered the pen and did a quick check of the animals. 'They seem to be fine. I think you've got foxes.' The owner nodded. 'I'll organise some baiting.' Rose interjected. 'Have you tried using chili pepper? Boil water, put it into a bottle, and spray it onto the llamas. That should work. Foxes hate chili.' Nic finished cleaning himself off. 'They should ban it, but what would happen to chilly-bin.'

This time, the farmer shook his head. 'Only in New Zealand do they call it a chilly bin. Here, we call them an esky. Are you from New Zealand?'

'No, bro. Born and bred in the state of Victoria.'

The farmer shrugged. 'I guess you were trying to be funny then.' Nic shrugged his shoulders. 'Been there, done that.' Polly then hurdled the fence, and the group returned to the car.

When they arrived the song 'Who Let the Dogs Out' by The Baha Men, was blaring from the radio, and Cadbury was woofing in time with the chorus. Polly put him on the leash and they headed towards a neighbouring property. 'The Shipping Containers we need to look at are located next door. It's only a ten-minute walk. We have to avoid the front paddock. It's where they keep the bull.'

Nic smiled. 'Don't worry, the bull charges as he doesn't take cash.' Polly looked at him. 'Stop it, Nic. If you're trying to be funny, it's not alarming.' Rose shook her head. 'I'm so sorry, Polly; I thought he would have grown out of it by now. He is nearly forty, you know.' Polly nodded. 'I know and I can't wait to tell his father about him.' Rose sighed. 'I thought you didn't know him.'

'I don't, but next time I have him in the car, I'll certainly let him know.'

When they reached the neighbours' front gate, it was closed and secured by a padlock. A decrepit sign was attached that read:

Trespassers welcome but beware the bull charges because he doesn't accept cash. Enter at your own risk.

Nic went up to the gate and pulled on the lock. 'Maybe they're not expecting us.'

Rose and Sandy stood back, waiting for further instructions; when Polly let go of Cadbury's leash, the dog leaped over the gate.

Nic soon followed the dog, scaled the fence, and called back to them: 'Are you coming? We need to get the dog back. It meets the rules of breaking and entering as we're in pursuit of our dog.'

'What about the bull?'

'Hey, animals love me. I'm sure we'll be fine.' Rose was about to climb the fence when she re-read the sign. 'You've been here before, haven't you?'

'No, well yep...but last time it was to work out how we avoid the bull. It's pretty simple; we moved him out of the paddock, and that's no bull.'

Rose stopped. 'Why are you so nervous? Is it because we shouldn't be doing this?' Nic turned around. 'We have permission. It's called a mortgagee sale. The group that owned this property has since vacated it and the auction in a couple of months. We're coming in to do an inspection.'

'But you didn't have the key to the lock on the gate.'

'Boy, you ask a lot of questions.'

Cadbury came bounding back to them and had something in his mouth. It was an old white bone, but he wouldn't give it up despite everyone trying to coax him to do so and evading everyone. Rose picked up a stick and waved it at the dog. 'C'mon boy, try this one. It's much tastier...' then threw the stick up in the air a few times and kept catching it.

As the dog got closer, Rose let the stick drop to the ground, and then, as Cadbury looked down, she grabbed him by the collar. Nic smiled. 'Who says you can't teach old dogs new tricks.' Rose looked at him. 'It's not a trick...it's called a substitution diversion. I'll try it on you one day.' Nic took the bone from Cadbury's mouth and examined it. 'Well, this isn't funny at all. It was part of someone's upper arm, but it's not the humerus.'

Sandy came up, and Nic handed it over. 'I guess we should call the Police then?'

'Not before we have a look around. We didn't realise it was a human bone, did we? This used to be a farm, and we ain't Doctors.' Sandy interjected. 'That's a bit thin. Polly is a vet, and I'm sure she knows the difference.'

'But Cadbury doesn't.' Nic returned the bone to Cadbury, and they all walked further along the rubble driveway until they found the homestead. It, too, had a large lock across the front door, and there was another sign:

Mortgagee in Possession. Do not enter.

Nic went up to the lock and pulled on it. 'Does anyone know how to pick a lock?'

Sandy, Rose, and Polly shook their heads, and Cadbury gave a woof as best as possible with a bone in his mouth.

Nic then took a small leather pouch from his pocket, extracted a key, and opened the lock.

'Never mind, this should work. Who knew a key was the best option?'

They entered, and the house smelled very musty. Papers and invoices littered the floor, along with rodent droppings. Nic commented: 'I don't think the cleaners have been here for a while.' Sandy looked around. 'How long has it been empty?'

'A couple of months.'

Rose shook her head. 'So, the shipping containers have been unattended here for a couple of months, but now we're here to investigate?'

'Not quite. The house has been empty, but according to the CCTV cameras, there's been quite a bit of activity at the farm. The big dirty rats have been coming and going.' Rose continued: 'I assume you're referring to people as rats, not rodents as rats.'

'Yep, and they knew where the cameras were, so there isn't much vision. It doesn't take much to turn off a camera if you have the right equipment and know-how. Not that I'd know anything about that.'

Rose shook her head. 'Were they pulling plugs? Surely that would be suspicious enough to raise a concern?' Nic pulled the pouch out again and extracted a small, black, pen-like tube. 'If they use an infrared illuminator like this one, the camera can't catch the movements at night.' Nic flashed it towards the nearest camera lens. Polly nodded. 'So, just like any good rat, they've been doing their best work at night. I've met a few love rats in my day, and they have the same M.O.'

Sandy smiled. 'I think that's the case for all of us. Some stay around for the morning after, and in Rose's case, you may have to marry one, but she got lucky as she divorced the little rodent three days later.' Rose shook her head. 'Let's not go there. Besides, we have the stuff to look into. I think there is a little more stuff to this scam, not just a few big rats. This is big scale rats, with many gnawing teeth and whiskers.'

Nic nodded again. 'OK. It's time to get down and dirty. We have to sort out what these papers show, if anything, and then head to the storage containers. Hopefully, the rats haven't destroyed all the evidence.'

The group collected the documents into piles, collated them by date if found, and sorted any other miscellaneous information related to the fraud. The most recent date was around two months ago. The process took around an hour, and they were exhausted and filthy once complete. Sandy went to the kitchen to wash her hands and found the water had been turned off. 'Where can we wash?'

Nic looked around and noticed the bathroom door was open. 'There might be water in the toilet. Try that.'

Rose called out. 'Don't be disgusting.'

'I mean, it runs on rainwater via a pump, whereas the kitchen water is on mains.'

'OK water-boy, how do we get the pump working? Is the power still on?'

Nic smiled and then disappeared through the front door. The lights came on, and the pump started chugging. 'The house runs on solar. When we walked in, I saw the Tesla Powerwall Battery, but I didn't think it would still be connected. Those things are worth a couple of thousand dollars second-hand. I would have thought they'd have taken it already.'

Rose nodded. 'Not unless they needed to keep the electricity on in case they wanted to keep coming back and needed access to water and electricity.'

Polly grinned. 'Great. Maybe the shower works then.'

Sandy yelled out from the bathroom. 'Don't bother; there's no soap, shampoo, or other washing stuff in here, not even a towel. Besides, I think someone has been sleeping in the bath. Maybe not someone, but something very hairy and muddy. It could've been a wombat.'

Polly came into the room and peered into the bath. 'I don't think the wombats could manage to open the doors. I would say it was a couple of possums playing possum.' Nic then called them back into the lounge room. 'There's nothing else here worth looking at, so how about we go container hunting? I've heard those critters can be very good at disguising themselves as big metal boxes.'

The group moved outside, where Cadbury was patiently waiting. He'd collected another bone, and again, it appeared human. The dog gave a little woof in case they hadn't seen it and dropped the bone at his feet. Nic nodded at the new find: 'Good boy. You've found another one. Can you show me where you're getting them from?'

Cadbury woofed again and bounded off, and Nic followed the dog. 'C'mon guys, keep up. Dem Bones, dem bones, dem dry bones might be worth looking at as they might all be connected.'

Polly picked up the new bone and caught up to them. 'This is human. I would say about twenty or thirty years old.' Nic finally caught up to Cadbury and stopped at what appeared to be an old wrought iron gate. It was encrusted in tiny white snails but was adorned by a sign that read: **Canto Family Cemetery.**

Polly called out. 'I don't think you should be going back in there.'

'I'm fine with it, Polly.'

'I was talking to Cadbury.'

The group moved into the small cemetery, and Nic nodded towards the excavator parked off to the side of the field. 'Wow, that's one way to dig up old bones, but please don't tell Cadbury.'

Rose moved over to the tractor. 'I assume you know how to drive one of these?'

Nic nodded. 'Well, the key to starting it is key, but these days, if the business purchases several pieces of equipment from the same manufacturer, they use the same key for all the machines. In case you're wondering, stealing heavy equipment is difficult as you can't put it into your pocket.'

'Do you have a key?'

'Not with me, but I can improvise if we need to. A flat-headed screwdriver can do the trick.' Nic pulled one out of his little bag, then moved towards a pile of broken gravestones. 'I'm not sure what's going on here, but I think the caskets should be buried, not left on top.' Cadbury gave another little woof, then sat down at an open casket. Polly moved over to him and put on his leash. 'Sorry, Cadbury, I think you've had enough today.'

In the meantime, Sandy was moving around the cemetery, counting the headstones and numbering the caskets. 'I'd guess at least ten caskets have been dug up, but why would they do it?'

Rose smiled. 'Maybe to bury something else.'

15

The group moved around the cemetery, closing any opened caskets and putting bones back where they could, and then a loud bang broke the silence. Nic raised his finger to tell the others to stop what they were doing and when they heard the second bang, Nic motioned that they should lower themselves into a crouched position. Cadbury followed the prompt.

Rose whispered: 'That sounded like a gun.'

Nic nodded. 'I think so, too.'

Polly moved towards Cadbury and unclipped the leash. 'As well as being a chocolate pointer, he's a gun dog too. Do you want me to let him go?' Nic remained standing and looked at his phone. 'Nope. I think we'd better move back to the homestead.' Sandy glanced at him. 'How do you know the gunshot didn't come from there?'

'My Spidey senses tell me it came from the other direction.'

Rose crab-walked towards Nic. 'Or is it that you just saw the vision of the gunman on a trail camera that's linked to your phone.'

'Yep, to that too.' Nic led them back to the homestead. They went inside and sat around a makeshift table made from CHEP pallets. 'I think we'd better stay here and wait to see what happens. A couple more cameras are along the main track from the cemetery so that we can watch for more exciting stuff.'

Cadbury started making whimpering noises and then scratched at the front door.

'I'm sorry, Nic, he needs to um...water the trees.' Nic nodded, so Polly let the dog out and they watched more of the vision on his phone while waiting for Cadbury to return. 'He or she is getting closer. It may be, he thought, as he's just stopped to take a ...well ...water the trees.' Nic held up the phone to show the others, and Sandy looked out the window. 'Do you think he'll come up here?'

'I don't know, but just in case, I might get ready.'

Nic moved away from the group and returned a few minutes later with a plastic replica of a bolt-action 303 gun. Nic pulled back on the lever and checked that it was empty. Rose looked at him. 'I thought you said you don't carry a gun?'

'Yep, that's what I said. I never said I didn't know how to use them. This one is about thirty years old but still works. Every farmer needs to know how to use one just in case.'

'In case of what? And in case you don't know, but you're not a farmer.'

Nic shrugged. 'It's an old one of my childhood. I secured it away the last time I was here. It doesn't fire bullets, and I lost the little rubber thingies years ago, so we might have to yell out 'bang, bang' if it comes to that.'

They each took a window and kept a lookout. Nic leaned back from his window. 'I think he's stopped. Something must have spooked him.' Sandy was still looking out of her window. 'Maybe he spotted us.' Polly carefully opened the front door, whistled, then called out: 'Cadbury, you can come back in now.'

The dog came bounding up the path again with something in his mouth; it appeared to be a prosthetic leg. Nic again pulled the vision up on his phone, and they watched as the gunman hobbled along the track, using the butt end of a double-barrel shotgun as a makeshift crutch. Polly stepped outside, collected the leg, brought it inside, and placed it on the table. 'Well, at least we know who it is. There's a sticker inside it with his name and address.'

Rose looked at it. 'Or it could be stolen, or it could be the name of his Doctor.'

'I guess you could be right, but who would steal a leg?'

'Someone that doesn't want to pay for it. They average around five grand.'

Nic looked at it. 'You know if you try to win a case about a missing leg, you might not have a leg to stand on.' Rose was about to respond when they heard another bang. 'I hope he unloaded the gun before he started walking with it.'

Nic scrolled through the surveillance camera vision on his phone. 'Nope, I would say not. I think we're going to have to find him and help him. It doesn't look good.' Nic re-hid the gun, and Polly again opened the door for the dog. 'Cadbury, find the man with the shotgun.' The dog bounded off with dogged determination.

The group followed the dog back through the cemetery and found an elderly man lying face-up in a Wattle bush. He sat up to look at them. 'Oh, Hi. I wondered whose dog it was. Did you bring my leg?' Polly handed it over, and they helped him stand up to put it back on, then he wobbled side to side to settle the leg back into place. 'I'm Gus from the property that backs onto this one. I come over here occasionally to check on the cemetery and pay my respects to my kin folk. There's been a lot of going on at the farm lately. I've been monitoring things.'

Nic nodded. 'Thanks, Gus. These are my associates: Polly, Sandy, Rose, and Cadbury. He's the leg poacher. What happened to the freight containers?'

'They took the last of them last night. Loaded them onto trucks and took them out through my property. I assume they gave up trying to bury them as they were too large.' The man hobbled over to the nearest tree stump and Rose helped him sit down. 'I think they were hoping the soft soil in the cemetery would help them to bury the containers of whatever they were trying to bury, but the soil around here is mainly thick clay and big rocks.'

Rose nodded. 'How long have you been watching them?'

'About four months. I had heard an almighty crash a couple of weeks ago, so I came over and saw that one of the containers had fallen off the back of a tray truck. They were trying to put a helicopter back into it, along with briefcases full of cash. I took some photos. Do you want to see them?'

Nic shook his head. 'Nope, not here. Can you manage to walk?'

'Sure.' Gus stood, flipped the shotgun over, and started using it as a crutch.

Rose looked at it. 'It's not loaded?'

'Nope. It hasn't worked for about twenty years.' Gus spun the gun around and showed them the rubber stoppers at the end of both barrels. 'I'm into re-purposing things.' Rose stopped walking. 'What about the gunshots we heard?'

'I heard them too. I assumed it was coming from your direction. I get a little lost at times. The shots could've been coming from behind me.'

Nic shook his head. 'It wasn't us. We're not carrying any guns.' Rose quickly interjected. 'Well, not that have any bullets.'

They were returning to the homestead when another volley of bangs rang out. Nic called them to get closer, indicating they should hurry a little. 'I think we'd better find out where they're coming from.' Gus stopped and took a few deep breaths. 'There's no one next door as they're off shearing sheep, and over the other way, the Watersons are on holiday. It could be that one of their kids has returned early.'

Sandy moved back to help Gus shuffle a bit quicker. 'Could it be the people that are trying to hide this stuff are coming back?'

Nic was about to respond when his phone rang. He stopped to take the call and held his fist to tell the others to stop. 'Yep. OK. Yep, I got it. We'll head there instead.' He disconnected and addressed the group: 'Gus, your work shed is on fire. That was my guy in Melbourne. He'd picked up the call on the local Police scanner.'

Sandy looked at him. 'Does Chewy monitor every Fire, Police and Rescue channel around Australia?' Nic shrugged. 'Nope, only the ones where we are working. Let's get moving. It's about a ten-minute walk to the boundary fence, then a five-minute drive.'

Nic broke into a jog, then called back. 'And hopefully, we get back before the shed burns down.' Gus nodded. 'It should be OK. I've installed sprinklers on the roof in case of a bushfire; one went through a few years ago. The water pumps will kick in.'

Around ten minutes later, the group made it to the boundary gate, clambered into the back of Gus's Triton Ute, and drove along the track towards his place. After five minutes, they'd arrived, and the shed was almost razed to the ground. The acrid smell of burnt timber and molten rubber filled the air. Rose went to a water hose nearby and turned it on, but no water came out. 'I don't think the pumps are working, Gus.' They heard another explosion, and a gas bottle flew upwards. It landed just by the parked Ute. 'Damn, that means my Bar-B-Que is on fire too.'

The fire was still burning when the local Community Fire Service truck arrived to extinguish the remainder of the flames. One of the attendants walked up to Gus, holding a bit of shrapnel from an exploded metal tank. 'It looks like someone has been taking pot-shots at your welding tanks.' Nic came over. 'At least we know what direction the shots were coming from and they weren't shooting at us.'

The CFS Officer handed him the metal shard. 'This is a big hole made by a large calibre rifle.' Gus examined it, then moved over to the shed to consider what could be salvaged; however, the skillion roof of the veranda collapsed onto the ground. 'I guess this means another insurance claim. I've only just got the money from those people with the recent floods.'

Rose took the shrapnel from Gus, rolled it through her hands, and then started photographing it with her phone. 'I'll email the pictures to Chewy to see what he can find out.'

Another explosion sent another gas bottle into the air, and the CFS Officer told them to move further away from the fire. He called over to Gus. 'Do you still horde the gas bottles making them into flower pots?'

'Yep, but they should all be empty. I ensure it before using my angle grinder to cut them in half. It can get a bit gassy and flamey otherwise.' Sandy pointed at the pile of gas bottles at the shed's side. 'There's about ten over there, uncut, and the fire is heading over there.'

'I haven't got to them yet. I'll find something else to make flower pots from.'

The Fire Brigade put out the grass fire before anything else happened, and Rose's phone chirped. 'Chewy says it was most likely an SR98 ex-Australian Army rifle, and by the size of the hole, they're about a seven-point six calibre. Big gun.'

Nic nodded. 'That's good.'

'Why?'

'Because it's likely to be registered. We can backtrace to see who has access to one around here.'

Rose looked at him. 'Is your gun registered?'

'Boy, you ask a lot of questions.'

The group moved away from the fire to let the professionals complete the task and went inside Gus's house. 'Sorry about the mess; the maid's been on holiday.'

Rose looked at Nic. 'Do you use the same maid?' Nic grinned. 'Maybe.' Gus asked the others to sit around a wooden dining room table. It had been made from recycled CHEP pallets.

Gus had sanded down and polished them, making them rustic furniture. Sandy looked around and noticed two lounge chairs made of the same salvaged timber. 'Did you get a special on the pallets? They're supposed to be returned to the supplier.'

'I found them when I looked at the mess they were making at the cemetery. I thought they wouldn't mind if I re-cycled them. I also found a folder of purchase orders in the rubbish pile, so I took that for safekeeping.'

Gus went over to a 'CHEP' credenza, pulled out a folder, and put it on the table. Nic flicked through it. 'OK. This is more than just a Bank scam; what we have here is a big bust-out.'

Rose shook her head. 'So, they've been leasing the equipment and on-selling to unsuspected buyers. Surely, the details are recorded on the Government's Personal Property Security Register, known by the acronym 'PPSR'. That should put a substantial hole in their plan, as the assets should be able to be tracked.'

'Not necessarily, Rose. The whole basis of any data entered into a computer system is the quality of input. It is known by the acronym 'GIGO.''

Polly agreed. 'We have that same issue with one of our locums: Garbage In, Garbage Out. He puts stuff into our reporting system that we don't even understand. But what's the issue here?' Nic continued: 'If they use someone on the inside to ensure the information is incorrect, they alter the registration details. For example, suppose they took a Rolls Royce for security and recorded the seventeen-digit VIN using a fake number. In that case, no one is wiser unless a second person verifies the information. It's not as foolproof as the authorities expected it to be.'

Gus interjected. 'I would assume that's what could be going on here and could explain the bundles of cash. If they've already on-sold on the equipment, it will only cause a bit of angst for the lenders. Anyway, I'm thirsty; how about a cuppa?'

Cadbury gave a little woof, and Polly put the kettle on.

16

Gus linked his camera to the computer and downloaded at least a hundred photographs of the property with and without the workers and with or without the shipping containers. The pictures showed the empty containers being delivered, where they were stored, what they contained when they were filled, and when they were removed. Everything was date stamped, and Gus had even set up an Excel spreadsheet to track everything and everyone involved.

Nic smiled at the quality and plethora of information. 'And yet you told me nothing happens around here.' Gus looked at him. 'I only started looking into this when you rang me about two months ago and told me you needed a house-keeper. By the way, thanks for the new phone, camera, and updated network. I've loved watching the Star Wars movies on re-run.'

Rose looked at Nic. 'You know, I still haven't seen any of those little films. Driver was about to set me up with a thermos of coffee and a box of matches to keep my eyes open so I could binge-watch them. We ran out of time…so disappointing.'

Nic was about to respond when Rose's phone rang. Rose looked at the caller ID. It was her mother. 'Oh, Oh, this isn't going to be good.' Rose stepped out of the room to take the call. 'Hello, Mother. What's happened?'

'I was just wondering if you've heard from Michael.'

Rose put the call on speaker and beckoned Nic to join her. 'Nic has just joined me. Why are you expecting him to call me?'

'I've had a phone call from Davide Reed. He's one of the Managing Partners at his Accounting Firm, and the office doesn't know where he is. Some money is missing and they want Father to go into their office to chat with them.'

'Why does that concern me?'

'I thought, seeing your friends with them….'

'I'm hanging up now, Mother.'

'OK, but if they call you.'

Nic leaned in. 'How much is missing, Jana?'

'He mentioned a hundred million and some-thing about cryptocurrency. I don't even know what that is.' Rose hung up and sighed. 'I hope we don't get called in to look into that.' Nic shook his head. 'Me either. They have tech experts that look into those big ones; it's well above my pay grade. We'll wait and see.'

Rose and Nic returned to the other room where Gus was trying to play fetch with Cadbury. 'This dog might be good at finding things, but he's lousy at the fetch.' Polly nodded. 'That's because he's a pointer, not a retriever.'

The group then sat around the television and watched the photographs, scrolling through while Rose jotted down notes. 'I've counted at least five briefcases; did they all contain cash?' Gus nodded. 'I assumed so and decided to bring one back here if it was needed for evidence.'

He moved over to the credenza, pulled out a black Samsonite briefcase, placed it on the dining room table and snapped it open. It was full of one hundred dollar notes. 'I reckon there are about ten thousand dollars in this one. It was the lightest one I could carry. I can afford to do up this place now.' Nic looked at him. 'Mate, do I have to remind you about my rules of finders/keepers? It doesn't apply in our line of work.'

'That's OK. I don't have much use for money anyway. I trade my stuff. It keeps the taxman away and the wolf from the door.' Sandy picked up a giant snow cone that had been re-purposed into a terrarium. It had a couple of Venus flytraps inside. 'Ah, the infamous Dionaea Muscipula. How much do you sell these for?'

'A large one like that goes for at least one laying chicken.'

Sandy smiled. 'Could I swap it for a couple of pieces of KFC?'

'What's KFC?'

'The Colonel, the bucket. You know Kentucky Fried Chicken. It's a fast-food franchise. There's one on Bungendore Road in Queanbeyan.'

'Never been there. The only fast food here is the rabbits, although I've never caught one. I grow my own stuff, and that keeps me happy. I'm a veggie, greenie, fruity loopy. Isn't that right, Cadbury?' Gus patted the dog on his head, and Cadbury gave a little woof in confirmation.

Rose shook her head. 'Exactly how long have you lived here?'

'About seven months.'

Rose noticed that Nic had given a subtle nod and looked at him. 'That's interesting, as about seven months ago, I talked to Chewy about investigating a leasing caper, and here we are on a farm next door to where the shenanigans have been happening. Is there something we should know, Nic?'

Nic nodded. 'Well, my Father needed to offset his taxable income. Besides, it is said, "Find something you love working at, and you'll never have to work a day in your life." Nic used his fingers to emphasise the quote.

Rose nodded. 'I thought he worked for the US Secret Service.'

'Who told you that?'

'Cadbury'.

The dog woofed again and Nic was about to continue when this time Sandy's phone rang. Sandy looked at the number, didn't recognise it and turned the ringer down. A couple of minutes later, it rang again. 'Yes, this is Sandy Fraser. Oh, no... When? OK, I'm currently interstate but can be there tomorrow.' Sandy disconnected. 'Um...that was the Royal Adelaide Hospital. My Father is in intensive care. He's got COVID.'

Nic stood up and came over. 'I'll get Polly to drive you to the airport and put you on the next plane. I assume you guys have all had your jabs?'

Rose tapped at her phone and brought up the Health app. 'Yes.'

Sandy and Polly did the same; Cadbury gave a woof, but Gus shook his head. 'As well as being an active veggie, greenie, fruity loopy, I'm also an anti-vaxxer. You have no idea what the government is putting into your arm when you get the jab. I've read they are shooting into your body, those little nanorobots that can keep track of you.' Sandy looked at him. 'Where did you read that?'

'On the internet. It's my go-to for truth in reporting.' Sandy continued: 'So Gus, as long as you don't leave this property for the next couple of months, years, or forever, and don't have anybody visit you and you continue to hideout from the world, you most likely won't catch COVID?'

'Exactly.'

"Well, sorry to burst your bubble, but my Father has just returned from Antarctica. He was involved in a research project there, and no one there had COVID. You could call that the ultimate in isolation. They have no idea how he caught it.'

Polly stood up. 'Each to their own. We'll go back via the hotel to grab your stuff, then head to the airport. The next flight to Adelaide is in an hour.'

Cadbury grabbed his leash and went to move outside with Polly. 'Stay here, Cadbury. I'll be back in about an hour.' The dog looked up at her with his puppy dog eyes. 'Uncle Nic will look after you. Who knows, he might even let you look for another bone.'

Sandy and Polly drove away, and Gus went to the 'medicine' cupboard. 'It's Happy Hour Time. Who's for a G & T, whisky, or wine?'

Nic nodded. 'Sure, I'll have one, but it's only four o'clock.'

'Really? I'm exhausted and missed my afternoon sleep. I need a fixer-upper.'

Rose stood. "I'll join you. What type of gin do you have, Gordons, Bombay Sapphire?' Gus shrugged. 'I make it myself. Use my juniper and my everything.'

Nic smiled. 'Just leave out the juniper and make mine a chai tea, not a G & T.'

Gus returned holding five bottles, each containing various flowers and leaves. 'This one is my favourite. I use whatever works; in this case, it's the flowers from the local weed garden.' Rose shook her head. 'Do you still have a license to run the still? It's illegal to operate one without a license.' Gus stopped in his tracks. 'Crap, what about all my beer and whiskey stills. Do I have to hide them too?'

Nic shook his head. 'Technically, you're a rectifier, which means you are de-distilling a neutral spirit and then introducing your botanicals. So, paying the applicable taxes is fine if you have a rectifier license. It's available free from the Australian Tax Office. You just have to register online.'

Gus looked at him. 'I've only just got onto the internet. I didn't know about that.'

Rose interjected. 'Ignorance of the law is no excuse.'

'Boy, you people are party poopers. What does that mean for Happy Hour?'

Nic smiled. 'We can use my license. This is my place, so technically, you're using my equipment.' Rose looked at Nic suspiciously. 'I thought this was your Father's place?' Nic smiled. 'It might have something to do with my Family Trust, so technically, it's mine.'

Gus was a little overwhelmed with all the tax stuff and made his drink a triple, then Rose took a long draw from her gin and stood up. 'This is good gin, Gus.' Gus nodded, and Cadbury gave a little woof. Rose continued: 'So Nic, are there any other occasions when you got a major heads up on investigation things and purchased things for tax purposes?'

Rose had used her fingers to emphasise her point about things, and Nic continued: 'Not really, but this one seemed too good to pass up. It's on mains water and power and comes with a live-in caretaker. I roll the dice and sometimes land on a property, but most of the time, it's just free parking, or I win ten dollars at the beauty contest.'

Rose tapped a few buttons on her phone and found a news item of interest regarding the recent farm sale. 'It says here the property sold at auction for two and a half million dollars, well over the reserve. How is that a good buy?'

'I never said it was a good buy; it was more a purchase of convenience. How was I to know something untoward was going on next door?'

'I assume you did your research?'

'And my next plan is to put a hotel on Mayfair if I can figure out the rules of Monopoly. I don't anybody understands how to win at that game.'

Rose nodded. 'Don't roll three doubles; otherwise, you end up in jail.'

Nic stood up and stretched. 'I think it's time I take Cadbury for a walk so he can water the trees.' Nic took hold of the dog's leash, and they headed outside.

Gus returned to the credenza. He removed his false leg, propped it against the side of the cupboard and poured himself another triple. 'Now that he's gone, how about we talk about the elephant in the room.' He turned around and leaned against the cupboard. Rose smiled. 'He's just left with Cadbury.'

'Not him, my missing leg.'

'Oh, that elephant. I wasn't going to mention it as I assumed you must be tired of people asking about it.'

'Not really. I can tell you it happened long ago in a far-off galaxy.'

'What's with you men and all the Star Wars references?'

'It's the little Yoda in all of us. I lost my leg when I was with the Forces fighting in Afghanistan. It's been about fifteen years. I haven't missed it at all.'

'I assume you're talking about the war and not your leg?'

'You catch on quickly, don't you? That's where I met Nic, too.'

Rose took a deep sigh. 'Is this something I need to know about?'

Gus turned around again, opened the top drawer, pulled out two medal boxes, and held it up upon opening the first box. 'It's an Afghanistan Service Medal. This one's mine.' Rose stood and moved towards him to take a closer look. 'You keep it in the top drawer?' Gus nodded. 'Yessiree. I don't think anyone will steal this one. The other thought might be more interesting.' Gus opened the second box.

It contained a Medal of Honour, and he handed it over to Rose. 'I didn't know any of these were in Australia. I thought they were only presented to US Soldiers.' Rose turned the medal over to read the inscription but couldn't quite make out the name; she brushed off the dust, and the gold bar across the back read: "THE CONGRESS TO CMDR NICOLAI THORN."

Rose carefully put it back into the box. 'Nic would have only been in his mid-twenties when in Afghanistan. Is this his?' Gus looked up. 'Nope. It's Nic's Father – Commander Thorn US Marine Corp.'

Rose lifted the medal again and held it up. 'So what you're telling me is that Nic's Father's name is Nicolai, and his two sisters are Nicky and Nicole. It must get very confusing at Christmas time.'

'Exactly, but what if they use those names for safety and family protection.' Gus was about to continue but Nic had returned from walking Cadbury. 'Did you miss us? We didn't get lost, although

I suspect Cadbury is a St. Bernard in disguise. He's quite a barrel of laughs. Hope you didn't run out of words to say to each other.'

Rose turned to face Nic, quietly putting the medal back in the box and silently closing the drawer behind her. 'Well, I am a little lost for words.'

17

Polly had been waiting in a line of traffic to make the right-hand turn into Pialligo Avenue to head for the airport. There had been an incident on the M23 so they'd been stuck for at least an hour. Finally, the traffic started to move, and Polly slowed down to see what type of accident had caused the delay. A heavy-duty forklift appeared to have fallen from the side of a tray truck and was only now being removed. The Police arrived to stop the traffic and direct the recovery crane to the site.

The cars continued to inch forward, and as they were now adjacent to the crash site, Sandy lowered her window to get a better view. They overheard a couple of men arguing. It was becoming raucous and physical, then a third man joined in. Sandy and Polly were so close they could not avoid over-hearing the conversation:

'Grunt, shut your trap and stop arguing. I told you to use the heavy-duty chains, not those crappy things you found on eBay. We've haven't got much time to get rid of all this stuff.'

The younger of the trio raised his middle finger, then gestured towards a second man: 'Well, Boof refused to have a shower. He still smells like dead people. It took me a whole bottle of that girly shampoo stuff to get the stink of the dead out of my pores. Now I smell like potpourri. We had to dig up the caskets, but why did he have to open them? There was nothing but dead people.'

The second man laughed, reached into his pocket, pulled out a small opaque plastic bag and waved it at him. It appeared to contain grey and white pebbles.

Sandy wondered what they were, and Polly leaned over. 'They look like teeth.'

The man opened the bag and dropped a few of the 'stones' onto the palm of his hand. 'One old codger had at least six gold fillings. His jaw remained intact, so I used my pliers to get them out. Damn, I left my box of tools there. It was your stupid idea to use that stupid label thing, too. Everything has got my name on it.'

This time, the young man laughed: 'What about the desecration of the dead and what if they come looking for us? They'll want their teeth back. I've seen The Walking Dead on Netflix. Zombies can kill.'

Boof looked at him. 'Grunt, you're idiot. These five little pieces of gold are worth about five hundred bucks. I've got about twenty and need to melt the metal off.'

Polly leaned closer to Sandy. 'I think we should take a picture of these guys just in case it means something.'

Sandy opened the app on her phone and started taking a few shots. 'Nothing means nothing until it means something you know. I've learnt that from Nic.'

'I've heard him say that. How long have you and Rose been working with him?'

'A while now. We were sitting around in Brisbane looking for something to do as our clothing shop had to be shut down when they built a new road. Now we get to travel around Australia and do something with him.'

Polly smiled. 'How many scams and fraud things have you busted?'

'We're up to about twenty or so. I lost count last year. It all started when we did that fraudulent invoice investigation at the Adelaide Motor Show. Rose has done a few without me.'

'Do you find him easy to work with?'

'We don't think it's working.'

'Oh, that's a shame. He speaks highly of you both.'

'Not working, working....it is working, but it's not working for us. We're having too much of a good time busting these dopes with their stupid scams. It's not working for us, but it all seems to work.'

'That sounds like something Nic would say.' Sandy nodded. 'We call it 'Nic Thorn Gobble-de-gook', and it took a while for us to learn. It was like another language.'

A police officer approached them and put his hands on the roof of Polly's car: 'Sorry, ma'am, it's going to be a while. The truck stopped suddenly and the forklift didn't, so it toppled off. Hope you're not trying to get to the airport.'

Sandy looked up at him. 'I'm supposed to be flying to Adelaide. The plane leaves in about half an hour, but I'll get the next one if I miss it. My Father is in the ICU at the Royal Adelaide Hospital with COVID. I'm trying to get there before...he um...they're saying it's a nasty bug.'

The Police Officer nodded, 'I'll see what I can do,' and returned to his motorbike to pick up the two-way. Sandy watched as he nodded a few times and looked back at her. He eventually hung up and moved back to them. 'Do you have any luggage?'

Sandy shook her head. 'No, just my handbag. I've got clothes at my Father's place in Adelaide.' He smiled and opened her door. 'Have you been on the back of a motorbike before?'

Sandy shook her head again. 'Nope, and I've never been inside a Police car or seen inside a jail. I've not had a parking or speeding ticket either. I like the band, The Police, though. I'll send an S.O.S. if I have to.'

The Officer smiled again. 'I've cleared it with my boss and have the approval to take you to the airport. Hop on the back.' Sandy stepped out, shut the car door, and leaned in through the window towards Polly: 'Wow, the Police in Canberra are so helpful.'

'It may have something to do with the corps diplomatique plates on the car and the US diplomat ID sticker on the front window.'

'Spoilsport.'

Sandy moved over to the motorbike and waited while the Police Officer removed the storage containers covering the back area, then folded down and clipped in a second saddle. 'My name is Officer Austin Bojanovic, and I'll be your driver today, but having diplomatic immunity doesn't stop you from having to wear a helmet. Where are you from? I can't pick up your accent.'

Sandy couldn't come up with a suitable response, so she used the classic movie line: 'If I told you, I might have to kill you.' The Officer smiled then handed over his business card to Polly. 'Please give me a call for anything. I can do other work, too.'

Sandy didn't miss the flight and in just over two hours, she was outside the COVID isolation unit at the RAH, trying to convince the attendants that having diplomatic immunity should allow access to her father. They didn't believe her, and after some convincing her to leave the hospital, she decided to take a tram to her Father's house in Glenelg.

Once settled, Sandy spilled the contents of her handbag onto the dining table and remembered they'd taken photographs of the three men, so she rang Nic. 'Polly and I ran into an accident on the way to the airport, but I still caught the plane thanks to a ride on a motor cycle, hugging the back of a Police Officer.'

'So I heard, and you have some pictures to send me, but how is your Father?'

'Not good. The ward has several people already succumbing to this virus, but he should pull through. He's tough and knows I'll never forgive him if he doesn't.'

'Did you tell him that?'

'I didn't get to see him, but I suspect he already knows. Anyway, have there been any further developments?'

'Only that Cadbury keeps finding more bones. A moment ago, he brought back a whole lower jaw. I thought we'd put them all back into the caskets.'

'Check the jaw for tool marks.'

'What? Why?'

'Well, if we're lucky, the pictures of three men I'm about to send you have one of them holding a bag of teeth.'

'And?'

'The teeth have gold filings. We overheard them saying he'd taken them from a bunch of corpses. Is that the phrase? Maybe a crypt of corpses? Anyway, he wants to extract the gold.'

'Well, that is interesting. Hopefully, we can get the bite on him.'

'Nic.'

'Yes, Sandy.'

'Will you guys be OK without me?'

'Sure, we have Cadbury to keep us in line if we're not, and speaking of Cadbury, he's found another bone. This one looks like a radius. We'd better find out where he's getting them from, as there might be another burial site. Have fun in Adelaide without us. Would you like me to have Driver come up from Victor Harbor to drive you around?'

'No, but thanks anyway. It might be best if no one moves around until they get a handle on the virus. I think I'll be staying down here for a while. They won't tell me when he will be well enough to come home.'

They disconnected, and Gus uploaded the photographs to the computer. Nic then moved over to Cadbury, collected the bone, and handed it to

Polly. 'This one also looks human. We'd better go for another walk before it gets too dark.'

The group gathered equipment to search outside, and Polly stepped onto the porch. 'Fetch dem bones, Cadbury, fetch dem dry bones.' The dog loped off, and all they swore was that it was smiling.

Sometime later, the dog returned with another bone, which appeared from an upper arm, although it was significantly degraded. Cadbury dropped it at Nic's feet, and the dog waited for a thank you. Nic picked it up. 'You know this isn't very funny at all.'

Rose looked at him. 'You've already used that line.'

'Sorry about that, but I might need to call a priest to re-bury every one of them. Burying people is not my thing.'

'Or we could just find out where Cadbury is getting them from and start our investigation, then we can call in a Minister to administer the last rites... again.'

'Yep, there is that.'

Polly called out. 'Fetch dem bones, Cadbury.' Cadbury headed off again with his tail wagging furiously and this time, the group followed him more closely, eventually arriving at a pile of bones. Nic shook his head. 'Someone must have sorted through them, as most parts had been separated into piles: Heads, tails, arms and putting the left and rights legs in and shaking them all about. It's a nasty thing they've been doing here.'

Rose looked down at the four piles. 'I assume you're referring to the desecration of the dead and not that you will need to re-bury them?'

'Yep, but no. At least they've helped the investigation, and that's a good thing.'

Nic put on some rubber gloves, leaned down, and opened a discarded toolbox. 'Well, isn't that just dandy? Whoever owns this stuff has labelled everything just in case it gets stolen. He mustn't trust the people he works with. Such a shame.'

Rose was now standing next to him. 'What happened to honour amongst thieves?'

Nic smiled. 'It only happens in the movies.' He carefully extracted a sizeable shifting spanner and turned it over in his hand. 'Well, when we find him or her, I'm sure they'll be happy to get these back.' Polly clipped the leash onto Cadbury. 'I guess we're looking for someone called 'Boof.'' Nic nodded. 'And for someone with a label maker as every tool in the box has a name label on the handle or the shaft.'

"This belongs to Boof. Hands Oof."

18

Despite their best attempts, their latest search bore no more information or relevance to the leasing investigation. It appeared that whoever had neatly piled the bones was only after the skulls and gold fillings. They carefully covered the piles in an old, discarded tarpaulin they found nearby, and it too had the "Boof" label. The group returned to the homestead, and Gus started assembling a makeshift Bar-b-que from the surplus of wooden CHEP pallets. 'This is another one of my ideas. A fully combustible cooker that gets re-cycled into kindling once we've finished cooking.' Rose set the wood alight. 'So, every time you cook something, you have to make another so you can cook something? Have you tried making one out of metal as you can re-purpose that into another bar-b-que when you've finished cooking?' Gus shook his head. 'Where's the fun in that?'

They finished lunch, went back inside and Nic opened the email from Sandy, printed off the pictures of the men and put the photographs on the table. 'Anybody wants to guess which one is Boof?'

Rose leaned in and pointed to the larger of the gentlemen. 'This one. The smaller guy is Grant or Grunt, but I don't know who the third guy is. Chewy has just sent me the details of who owns the forklift, so that may be a lead, and a property search will tell us where we could go with that part of the investigation. You said it was a forced sale by the Bank, so they must be dealing with someone, somewhere.' Nic nodded. 'Unless they can't find them.'

'Who would walk away from getting the surplus proceeds from a property sale?'

Nic grinned. 'Someone that doesn't want to be found or has been making more money selling equipment, that they aren't entitled to either.'

Gus was standing at the kitchen sink tidying this up. 'Boof and Grunt look like someone that suits that description, but they are only two. I've got more photographs of other people. There were about six of them. At least we can start putting names to the narratives.' Gus moved to the computer to add another column with recent names to the spreadsheet.

Rose moved up and looked over his shoulder. 'It looks like you've already got names for some of them. Did you overhear something?' Gus continued. 'The guy kept twirling a knife and throwing it at anything that moved. I called him 'Mack'…and another guy I called 'Tuit' as he was always sitting around doing nothing.'

'Why Tuit?'

'He kept saying, 'Leave it. I'll get round to it when I'm good and ready.'

Nic pointed to the description of the fifth person. 'And this one?'

'I called her Phoney, as she was always on the phone. I think she was the main money man or woman, as the case may be. The others turned to her when they had a question.' Gus raised his hands from the keyboard. 'I've still got one left unnamed. I never heard him talk and never saw him walk. He only ever drove the car. I was going to call him Driver, but thought it might be too confusing for you guys, given you use that name already.'

Nic nodded. 'Let's call him The Driver anyway. I'm sure we won't confuse him with our Drivers. He does look familiar, though. Do you have any better photos?'

'Nope. He never got out of the car. He was very careful. He often spoke to Phoney, so maybe they're best buddies.' Gus updated the name, saved it, and shut the computer down. 'What's next?'

'We go for a drive. A de-registered company owns the property, but the ASIC search still listed the Director. They might deny everything, but you never know unless you go.'

Rose, Nic and Polly went outside to the Holden Statesman and drove towards Tuggeranong. It was about twenty minutes west of Queanbeyan. Polly lowered the privacy panel to talk to Nic, sitting with Rose in the rear. 'Where are we going once we get there?'

'Head for Homeworld. It's in the CBD. We'll have lunch at PJ Reilly's, then work out things from there. There is a heavy equipment distributor that we need to visit. It's about a ten-minute walk. The de-registered company was based at their office.'

They had lunch, and Rose brought up the location of the impending visit. 'I used 'Google Earth' to check out the distance. It's longer than a ten-minute walk, more like thirty. Why aren't we taking the car?'

'I want to walk off lunch.'

'I don't think so. What aren't you telling us?'

'I don't think it would be a good idea to use the Statesman with the corps diplomatique plates for a surveillance job? It's a little conspicuous.'

Polly smiled. 'We should have brought the Ute. How about I park around the corner and wait for you guys to do your thing?' Nic nodded. 'OK, but how about you take off one of the tyres and pretend you've got a flat.'

"It might work as long as the paparazzi don't see me. They like to poke fun at diplomatic cars that have any car trouble. It's one of their games to take pictures instead of offering assistance.' Polly parked the car in a side street and placed a paper sign on the dashboard:

"Diplomatic Immunity. Official Diplomatic Business."

Rose looked at it and smiled. 'That looks like a card that Nic uses; only his has 'Official Police Business' on it.' Polly nodded. 'I print them off at home. I'll wait in the car with the engine running, just in case.'

Nic smiled and then started to walk away. 'Keep your phone handy too. Rose, are you coming?' They walked around the corner to the site, but the gates were closed, and a paper sign was attached. It read: '**Back tomorrow.**'

The premises were otherwise devoid of machinery apart from a large wooden crate with a paper label: '**Do not open.**'

Rose shook her head in dismay. 'This is getting ridiculous.'

The trio returned to Queanbeyan, where Gus had prepared an early dinner. They went through the knowns and unknowns about the leasing case. It was now quite an extensive list. Gus had even called a forensic bone expert he knew, and she'd agreed to meet with them in the morning.

19

At about six a.m. and the sun had not yet risen. Cadbury was whimpering at the door, then he began to snarl. The commotion had awakened Nic, who was now trying to appease the distressed dog. 'Come on, boy, it's too early to be snarly. What's up?' The dog put his paws on the front door and lowered the snarl to a guttural growl. Rose joined Nic at the door. 'I think he's got the scent of someone or something.' Nic opened the door, and Cadbury took off at a great gallop.

Rose grabbed the leash, and they ran after him. Cadbury stopped and lowered himself to the ground as he entered the cemetery site. He was watching three men move around in the early morning light. Nic and Rose joined him in the undergrowth.

Rose whispered. 'They are the three men Sandy sent us the photos of.'

Nic nodded, and Cadbury gave a soft woof. 'I think we'd better stay here and not interrupt them. We don't know what they are up to, and they could be armed.' Nic kept himself low, moved closer while Rose and Cadbury did the same. 'Stay put, Rose. I'll see if I can get closer. Keep a hold on Cadbury.' Nic again moved towards the group, trying to listen in on the conversation, then removed his phone from his pocket, pressed record and held it in their direction, but he still wasn't close enough.

Rose realised what Nic was trying to do, so she removed her phone, pressed record, looped it through Cadbury's leash, and whispered into the dog's ear. 'Get closer, Cadbury. Find out what they are saying.' The dog slinked off and headed towards the group of men. Their conversation was breaking the early morning silence: 'Boof, there's nothing left here. What did we come back for? Are you sure you left your tools behind?'

'The Boss told us to recheck and ensure we've left nothing behind. I can't find my tools, but I'm sure I left them here, and we've lost a briefcase of cash somewhere.'

Boof suddenly stopped talking and indicated to the others they needed to lower themselves. 'Quiet, something is moving near the gate.' Mack and Boof squatted down, but Grunt remained standing. 'It's just that stupid dog. He kept stealing the bones after you took the dead people's gold. Do you want me to shoot it?'

Boof nodded and leaned down to a gun bag where he extracted an Army rifle, but in the meantime, Grunt had pulled a handgun from a holster behind his back. 'Let me do it.'

Rose gasped softly about a hundred metres away then looked for Nic but couldn't see him amongst the dense foliage. 'Damn you, Nic.'

Grunt cocked his Glock and tried to get a bead on the dog. 'I've been waiting for the day I can shoot something moving. I only get to practice on bottles, and they don't tend to move much.'

Fortunately, as Cadbury was shielded by the undergrowth, Grunt took a shot and missed by three metres, but as he had turned the gun sideways to make his aim, the recoil bit into the fleshy part between his thumb and forefinger. The weapon dropped into the dirt. 'Crap, that always works in the movies.'

Boof laughed and loaded his rifle. 'I bet I can't miss it with this little beauty.' He aimed, but then a phone started ringing. 'Turn that off. It's spoiling my focus.'

'It's not mine. It's coming from the dog.'

They watched Cadbury turn in a circle, apparently confused why his collar was ringing. The dog disappeared and the ringing stopped so Gus lowered his rifle. 'I guess he took the call.'

Rose decided her best defence was a retreat, so she scampered through the scrub and away from the group, but Nic was still nowhere to be seen. Rose returned to the homestead, and Gus and Polly were standing on the front porch waiting for her. Polly called out. 'We heard a gunshot.' Rose took a breath. 'The men returned this morning looking for the tool bag. One of them took a shot at Cadbury. Is he back here ?'

'Nic and Cadbury are having breakfast in the kitchen.'

Rose opened the front, entered the kitchen, and found Nic feeding Cadbury a piece of toast. Nic smiled and threw her phone over. 'Good idea with the phone, but there was no point in giving it to Cadbury as he only knows how to use an Android. He can't get used to the upwards swiping thing.'

Rose approached Nic, double-fisted into his chest and patted Cadbury on the head. 'Damn you, Cadbury. Where were you? I didn't call out as it may not have been a good idea. Did we catch any of their conversations?'

'Nothing, as they were too far away. I was about two minutes behind you. Boy, you can run fast. At least we know they've been, so now we only have to find out where they're going.'

Polly and Gus then entered the kitchen to join them in having breakfast, and they gathered around the computer to update the knowns and unknowns.

20

About two hours later, there was a knock at the door. Polly went down the hall and returned with a woman in tow dressed in a white HAZMAT suit, including a full face mask. The woman nodded to the group and removed her headpiece. 'Hi, I'm Bonita, and I believe you have a bone problem?'

Nic stood up and shook her hand. 'Thanks for coming. Yep, we have a real boney problem so we need someone official looking at the old cemetery site without raising suspicion.' Rose realised the woman's name may be a fake. 'Nic, I think you could come up with a better name for a forensic pathologist than "Bone-Eater." The woman held out her hand. 'And you must be Rose.'

Bonita unzipped the white suit and sat down, then nodded at Gus. 'What's the latest on the bones at the cemetery?' Nic continued: 'Cadbury was shot at this morning.'

Rose shook her head. 'We were all shot at this morning. We were lucky that those guys can't shoot straight.' Nic smiled. 'Well, that's at least one thing in our favour.'

The group gathered around the computer, updated a few items, and then Gus printed out the spreadsheet so they could each be allocated a part to summarise. Rose finished first. 'I would assume that Chewy could get the real names of these men by running an association and identity app. That might fill in a few gaps.'

Gus nodded. 'He's already done it and emailed it to me this morning. I was going to update the names, but I thought it would be easier to leave them as they are.'

Nic smiled, then added: 'And we've got the Bank guy sorted out now, too. I knew an insider would manipulate the registration details to invalidate the data. If we can't check the serial numbers against the equipment, it will be hard to verify which is what. He's of the Bankers I've been talking to. His name is Scott Free.'

Polly then referred to her list of equipment that Gus had photographed. 'Chewy has discovered where the equipment sales originated. Most of the heavy equipment was purchased through a company called BY Equipment Traders, and according to the business name search, the initials 'BY' stands for 'Big Yellow.''

Rose leaned in. 'And I assume the business is no longer trading, and the ASIC search shows no one listed as the current business owner.'

Bonita smiled. 'You catch on quickly, don't you, Rose?'

Rose nodded. 'I guess that means we're about to head off to hunt down a Banker.'

Gus referred back to his notes. 'I think we've missed our chance there. Chewy used his contacts with QANTAS, and managed to find him. The Banker is booked on the next plane flight from Canberra to Singapore. It leaves in about an hour.'

Cadbury gave a loud woof, and Polly looked down at the dog. 'I guess that means he's either hungry or has an idea.'

Cadbury woofed again, then scampered towards Sandy's jumper that she'd left in the car in her haste to get to the airport. The dog gathered it in his mouth and came back to the table.

Polly nodded. 'Of course. Good job, Cadbury.' Polly then went to her handbag and retrieved a business card, made a call, and it was answered quickly: 'This is Officer Bojanovic. How may I assist you?'

'Hello, Officer Bojanovic. This is Polly Anner. You gave me your card when you took my friend Sandy to the airport on your motorbike. Are you still in Canberra?'

'Yes, ma'am.'

Polly put the call onto speaker. 'I would like your assistance to retain a flight leaving for Singapore. Can you help?'

'I'm at the airport at the moment. I'm part of the service providing safety to a 'one-name' pop starlet. How is Ms Sandy? Did she make the connecting flight to London to meet with the American Secret Service people? She mentioned someone called Thorn.'

'Yes, she did, and thank you for your assistance. However, I need your assistance to locate one of my agents, 'Scott Free.' He is on the flight. He will be in the economy class section, but I forgot to give him the First Class upgrade. I'm sure he'll appreciate it. The carrier is refusing to help me as he has already boarded.'

'Certainly, but can't you upgrade via the phone app?'

'Nope, they are being held at the departure gate. Are you able to collect them and have someone board the plane?'

'I'll see what I can do.'

The call was disconnected and Polly went over to Cadbury to give him a big cuddle. 'Who says only Lassie comes up with good ideas to save the day.'

Meantime, Nic called the airport and managed to delay the flight by calling in a favour and soon the Flight Captain was making an announcement over the intercom: 'I'm sorry, ladies and gentlemen. We have a slight delay before taxiing to the runway. We won't be more than ten minutes. Please don't be alarmed. We will be re-opening the forward door as our Flight Marshall needs to come aboard.'

Somewhere in the middle aisle of business class, a man was becoming a little agitated and called to the attendant: 'How long until we are in the air? We are late already.' The attendant smiled. 'Only a couple more minutes, Sir. Please remain sitting and keep your seat belt fastened.' The man raised himself from his seat, looked forward and saw the Air Marshall board the plane; took a deep breath and lowered himself down. The attendant then met with the air marshal, and they both turned around to look further down the plane. The anxious man looked up and caught the eye of the Marshall, then unclipped his seatbelt and stood up to open the overhead cabinet. 'Please remain seated, Sir.'

The man ignored the request, pulled down a black briefcase, spun the combination to check the lock and stepped into the aisle. 'I have to get off. Let me off.' He considered his options, then realised that the only open door exit was forward, but he could use the plane's length to his advantage to exit from the rear. He turned and ran, dodging the grasping hands of the other stewards and fellow passengers, and made good headway until a burly gentleman stood in his way: 'Come on, mate. We're all running late. Now sit down and behave.'

The decamping man clobbered him with the suitcase, it sprung open, and bundles of cash were strewn amongst the surprised passengers. It was bedlam. He then used the chaos to reach an emergency exit door, pulled down the panel, activated the escape shute, jumped on, and slid down to the tarmac below.

Polly's phone rang at the homestead: 'It's Officer Bojanovic again. I'm sorry he may have injured himself when he jumped from the plane. He was trying to run away.' Polly smiled, and the Officer continued: 'He activated the escape hatch and jumped on, but we caught up with him.'

'Did he say anything?'

'Not really, although he wondered who had paid for upgrading his ticket to First Class, and he said he'd never heard of you.'

Nic overheard the comment and smiled. 'One down, five to go.'

21

In the morning, Nic, Rose and Polly decided to test their luck and drove back to Tuggeranong, but the gates were locked again. This time, the paper sign read: "Gone for breakfast. Back in Five."

Rose and Nic were considering their next move when a young man came up behind them. 'Sorry, I was getting my morning coffee. I have to close the office as I'm the only one here. My Boss has taken an urgent leave of absence. I'm Bourne. How can I help?' Nic nodded, retrieved a photograph of Scott Free from his pocket, and then held it up for the young man to inspect. 'Do you know this man?' Bourne nodded. 'Yes, that's my Father. What has he done now?'

Rose was about to respond when Nic put his hand on her arm. 'Nothing. We were just wondering if we could hire some heavy equipment. We were recommended to come to this place, but you are out of stock.'

Bourne looked at him suspiciously. 'We only provide to a limited number of clientele. Who recommended us?'

'A couple of stragglers. I don't know their names, but they were working next door to my property in Queanbeyan.' The young man took a step backward, and Nic assumed he was about to make a break for it. 'I'll pay cash. Do you have anything I can use? The matter is urgent.'

Nic folded out a wad of hundred-dollar notes, waved it at him and Bourne changed his composure. 'I've only got a forklift and a bulldozer left.'

'Are they here?'

'Out the back.' Bourne unlocked the gate and led them across the vacant lot towards a warehouse. Nic nodded toward Rose. 'Will it be OK if my friend stays here?' Bourne nodded, and Nic leaned towards Rose's ear to fake a kiss on her cheek, then whispered. *'Give it ten minutes, then call out: This is a Police Raid.'* Rose stopped walking. 'Sorry, Bourne, do you have a toilet I can use?'

'Sure, there's one in the office.' Bourne threw over the keys. 'Let yourself in.'

Bourne and Nic continued towards the warehouse while Rose went to the office and began searching the area after ensuring Nic and Bourne were not in view. A three-door filing cabinet was off to one side; as it was locked, she went through the drawers and found a key. Rose open the drawer and removed a file, then realised they were the original sales dockets from all the equipment, including the helicopter. She was taking photographs but was abruptly interrupted by a large shadow behind her. 'What the hell do you think you're doing?'

Rose turned to face the voice and immediately recognised the woman from the photographs. It was Phoney.

'I'm taking pictures.'

'Don't get smart with me, young lady. Who let you in here?'

'Bourne. He is showing my friend some of your heavy equipment. We want to hire it to do some farm work.'

'I don't think so.'

'If you don't believe me, we can find them.'

The woman looked at Rose. 'I think you'd better sit down and wait. I'll go and find them myself.' Rose sat on the chair behind the desk and watched the woman go to a box on the floor, where she extracted a length of rope. 'Now play nicely while I tie you up.'

Rose took a sigh. 'I promise not to move. You don't have to tie me up.'

'Shut up. I'm thinking. Who told you to come here?'

Rose decided to change her tact. 'Two fat, dumb guys that couldn't properly secure a forklift to a tray truck. The stupid idiots caused a major traffic jam the other day and almost made my friend miss her flight to Adelaide to see her Father. He has COVID...and he...'

'Shut up.'

'No, I won't shut up, and my friend has to deal with re-burying several dead people. Who would ever think extracting gold filings from dead people was a good idea?' The woman sneered at her. 'I said shut up.'

'Besides, one of your cohorts took a shot at our dog.'

Phoney moved around the desk to get closer and raised her hand to slap her. Rose closed her eyes in anticipation then overheard an announcement: 'This is a Police Raid.' Two Police cars entered the premises with lights flashing.

The driver stepped out and moved towards the office, waving a piece of paper: 'This is a search warrant for these premises. Stop what you are doing and immediately exit the office.'

Rose stood up and looked at Phoney. 'My name is Rose Palmer, and my friend Nic Thorn was brought in to investigate this scam that you and your Banking mate, Scott Free, are running. He's already in custody, which might explain why he's not talking to you. He might be tied up.'

A door opened at the back of the office, and Nic stepped through with Bourne following him. Rose smiled when she noticed the plastic ties around the young man's wrist and that he appeared to have a stomach problem. Nic shrugged. 'I can't believe this guy. First, he doesn't like me making fun of his name and then tells me to sit on a cold concrete floor while he finds something to tie me up with. I gave him a little tickle in the ribs to remind him to respect his elders.'

Rose smiled. 'Bourne, son of Scott...that makes you Bourne Free. Were your parents fans of the movie about lions?'

Bourne looked at her. 'I was named after Jason Bourne, the super sexy ex-spy guy.'

Rose shook her head. 'You might need to check your facts. Born Free was a 1966 movie about an abandoned lion cub in Kenya. Are you sure you're not adopted? Besides, there's only room for one sexy, super ex-spy guy in my life.'

Polly entered the office, assisted Rose into the Statesman, and offered her a water bottle. 'How did you know Nic was talking to me about the Police Raid?'

Rose smiled. "I knew he was up to something as he's never kissed me on the cheek. The earbuds work well, don't they?'

Polly smiled. 'I think we can mark off another two from the list. Phoney and Tuit.'

Nic and Rose arrived back at the homestead about an hour later, and Cadbury bounded up to them with something in his mouth. The dog dropped it at Nic's feet; this time, it didn't appear to be a human bone. Nic picked it up and gave the end a nibble. 'That's a relief. This tastes like a dog biscuit.'

Gus came up a few moments later, wiping his hands on an apron. 'I think I've found a new hobby, making doggy delights. It beats the repurposing thing.'

Rose smiled. 'Have you tried it on any other dogs?'

'Not yet, but Bonita reckons they look good enough to eat.'

They moved inside, and the kitchen was awash with a moist, meaty, doggy biscuit smell, and it was disgusting. Rose immediately turned around and headed for the front door. 'It smells of a combination of wet dog and old shoes. I think I'll stay out here for a while.'

A couple of moments later, the others joined her outside. Nic brought out the laptop computer so that they could update the names, then his phone rang. it was Chewy with an update, so Nic took a big gulp of air, stepped back inside and returned moments later. 'Scott Free is trying to get bail. It's doubtful, given that this fraud amounts to around two million dollars in equipment and cash. Once we match the equipment to the correct VIN, we can link it together. A search warrant was served on a hangar at the airport, where they re-covered five more briefcases containing cash. We're scheduled to meet with the Fraud Squad at Police HQ tomorrow at two, just before the arraignment.'

Polly nodded. 'What about the bones? Do we have to put them all back?'

'I guess so.' Cadbury sat down despondently and leaned forward onto his paws. Nic continued: 'We still have to track down Boof, Grunt and Mack. Has anyone got any ideas?'

Rose smiled. 'We could put an ad on Gumtree that we have a bag of tools to give away. The only issue is that they have a name label on them.' Nic nodded. 'I'll get Chewy onto it or round to it, as the case may be. Oh, by the way, Rose, that's the first time I've heard you refer to me as a super sexy ex-spy guy.'

Rose shook her head. 'What I said was Jason Bourne was the only sexy, super ex-spy guy in my life.'

'You said 'in this room.''

'Nope. You need to have your ears checked; you're nearly forty you know.'

'But you're closer to thirty than I am to forty, and I haven't received an invitation to your party yet.'

'I would have sent it by mail, but I never know where you are.'

Polly shook her head. 'What are you guys talking about?'

Nic smiled. 'Rose turns thirty next month and hasn't invited anyone to the party.'

'Oh, is that all? 'When is your birthday, Rose?'

'I can't remember.'

'It will be on your Driver's Licence.'

'I've forgotten where that is, too. I hate getting old.'

Nic was about to respond when Cadbury stood up, and the hackles along his back began hackling. The dog took a big sniff of the air and started to run down the path. Polly started to chase him. 'I think someone's coming up the drive, and Cadbury is unhappy about it.'

The group watched as the dog reached the gate and sat down. He began growling at the car stopped at the entrance just as three men stepped out. One of them was brandishing a rifle.

22

The man held up the rifle, looked at Nic, took aim at Cadbury and loudly stated: 'I won't miss this time. We're here to collect something you have of ours.' Nic stopped the others from coming any further and whistled to Cadbury. 'You can come back now. The nasty man, with the nasty gun, won't hurt you.'

Cadbury gave a guttural growl, turned, and headed back. Polly looked at the trio and whispered to Nic. 'I assume that we are in the presence of Grunt, Mack and Boof and I guess he wants his tools back?'

Nic shook his head softly. 'More likely the brief-case of cash.' Nic called out to them: 'I'm not sure what you think we have, but we're just the nice neighbours that live next door. Nothing less, nothing more. What do you think we have?'

Boof lowered the gun. 'If you're such nice neighbours, how about you let us in. We can have a nice cup of tea and a piece of cake and talk about it.

Nothing less, nothing more.' Nic contemplated the position and decided it would be best to keep the upper hand. 'Sure... We've got herbal tea, Lipton tea and G & T.'

The three men opened the gate and followed Nic's group to the homestead.

As the trio arrived, Nic realised that having access to their guns inside the house might not be ideal. 'Guys, would you mind leaving those things on the porch?'

Boof smiled. 'As long as you don't do anything stupid. You're not stupid, are you?' Nic shook his head. 'No, I'm Nic and this is my dog, Cadbury.'

Boof leant his rifle against the side of the front entrance. Grunt removed his holster, lowered his gun carefully to the wooden deck and Mack shrugged. 'I don't carry.'

The group entered the house, which still had the aroma of meaty dog biscuits, and sat at the dining table. Boof noticed his bag of tools on the floor. 'So, you've been to the cemetery?' Nic nodded. 'It's not our fault. The dog kept bringing us bones you'd dug up, so we had to look.' Boof pulled the bag of teeth from his pocket. 'Yes, and this little cache will make me money now that the job has collapsed thanks to you guys, but that's not why we're here.'

Gus kept stirring the bowl of brown mushy muck and Grunt sniffed the air: 'What the hell are you cooking? It smells like …dog.' Cadbury stood up, gave a woof, and Gus continued stirring. 'It's my special brownie biscuit recipe.'

'Well, stop. Otherwise, Mr Bang Bang sitting outside will make his presence felt.' Grunt raised his hand, made a 'gun' shape, and pointed at Gus, who was folding the batter into a metal tray. 'Almost done, then you can try one.'

Mack looked at him. 'You know, I make them too. Make sure you add a layer of Nutella in the middle.' Boof glared at him. 'Shut up.' He put both hands on the table. 'OK, this is the situation. We know Scott is in the slammer pending a court hearing later today, and Fiona and Rowan have been arrested, so we want your help to get our stuff. What's owed to us.'

Nic nodded. 'I assumed you were here for the briefcase.'

Boof grinned. 'We want that too, but you'll help us get them all back. Fiona rang and told me the cops missed looking in the wooden crate in the yard. We want you to break in and retrieve our stuff.' Rose shook her head. 'Not likely,' however, Nic responded differently: 'Sure. When?'

Boof grinned and looked at Rose. 'How about now, and we'll take the little lady with us so you don't do anything stupid.'

The trio of men stood up, went outside, gathered their guns and were about to walk toward the gate when Gus came hobbling out of the house with a container of chocolate brownies. 'Take these for your trip.' Mack opened the box, immediately took one and put the whole piece into his mouth. 'You added the Nutella. They're great. Take a bite, Grant.'

Grant slapped his hand away. 'Stop it. I'll have one later.'

Nic approached Rose, hugged her, and said loudly, 'You'll be safe. They need us, but don't eat the brownies; they're not good for you and will make you even fatter than you already are.' Boof looked at him. 'Wow, if I said that to my girl, I'd get slapped.' Nic shook his head. 'She's not my girl; she's my sister, Fatima.'

Mack, Boof, Grunt and Rose climbed into their car and waited for Nic and Polly to get into the Ute.

The drive to Tuggeranong took twenty minutes, and Rose ensured the men chowed down on the delicious brownies along the way. By the time they'd arrived, they all felt a little overdosed on chocolate. Nic and Polly had come and stood at the equipment site's gates. Nic pulled at the lock. 'Do you have a key?'

'Not likely. You're going to climb over.'

Nic looked up at the height of the perimeter fence. 'Do you have a ladder?'

Boof looked at him again. 'And yet you said you're not stupid.'

Polly jangled the car keys. 'I'll drive the Ute closer. We'll climb on the roof and then jump over.' Nic nodded. 'That'll work, but we'll all do it. You stay with the car, Polly.' Nic looked at Boof. 'I don't want you three claiming that we stole the stuff, so we're all doing it.'

Polly reversed the Ute into the space, and the men took turns climbing onto the roof and scaling the fence. Nic was first over, so he draped cardboard over the wall to make it easier for the others and made a pile inside the yard to land on. Mack was the last one to leap, but when he landed, he bent over and started taking deep breaths. 'Wow, maybe the fourth piece of brownie was too much. I think I'll wait here for a while. You guys go.'

Mack leant his arm against the fence and held his stomach. 'I think I'm going to be sick.' He wasn't just going to be as he did and then threw up. He then leaned against the fence, trying to keep everything under control. It wasn't working.

Boof shot an angry glance at him, and then the remaining three moved towards the large crate, and he looked at Nic. 'Open it.'

'With what.'

'I don't care. Use your head.' Grunt laughed. 'Use your.....' He felt for his stomach, and then he vomited too. 'What was in the brownies?' He leaned against the side of the crate and started taking deep breaths.

Boof smiled. 'I only had one, but I have a cast iron stomach. I can eat anything.' Nic waited, then heard the noise he was waiting for. It was coming from Boof's stomach, and he vomited too. Boof gasped in pain. 'Just what did he put in them?

Nic smiled. 'Acepromazine.'

Grunt called out between shudders. 'They use that to put sick animals to sleep.'

'Yep.'

'It shouldn't make you throw up.' Grunt vomited again.

'Nope. Not unless it's mixed with something else. Didn't you notice the lovely oleander hedge along my driveway? You might start feeling sleepy now as the acepromazine takes effect, but at least you'll stop vomiting.'

Nic looked over at Mack who was propped up against the fence and fast asleep.

Meantime, Rose and Polly had managed to open the gates and ambled up. 'Wow, Rose, another thing you've been working on. Picking a lock.'

Rose smiled and held up a large snap-lock punch. 'Not quite. I saw this in Boof's toolbox and wondered what it was.'

Polly looked at the three men splayed in various positions across the yard. 'I saw what Gus was mixing in but didn't think it would do that.' Boof managed to look up at her, trying to retain consciousness. 'You...with all your self-righteous...

stopping...making us... You make me sick.' Polly nodded. 'Well, Grunt took a pot-shot at my dog.' Boof smiled, then mumbled between gulps of air. 'He missed on purpose,' then fell into a deep slumber.

Rose looked at Nic. 'What do we do now? Get some buckets, sponges, and a large water hose?' Nic shook his head. 'Nope, the Police and the Fire Brigade are already on their way. We've got to get back and get ready for the court appearance at two o'clock. But how about we see what's in the wooden crate?'

Rose moved towards the crate and noticed the padlock was ajar. 'It's already open. Have you peeked already? I assumed it's empty.'

Nic smiled. 'Not quite. Open it and take a look.'

Rose leveraged the door open and peered inside. It was empty. 'I thought you said...' Nic nodded. 'Step inside. Watch out for the mirrors.' Rose took a step inside, and her foot was impeded. 'What is this?'

Nic smiled. 'It's your fault. When you told me how that car went missing in Mildura, I thought I'd try it using mirrors. The Police found the cache hidden behind a false wall in the crate. So I arranged them to leave it there and hide it behind some mirrors.'

'How did you think how Boof would react when he realised it was gone?'

'I might've accused his colleagues of removing the stuff, and if that didn't work, I might've smashed the glass, but none of that mattered as they're sleeping it off.'

The trio waited for the Police to arrive, and then Nic had to subtly explain the reason for using a noxious plant mixed into the brownies. The Police wanted to know what happened to the remainder of the batch in case it was needed for evidence. Rose presented them with the empty container. 'They ate them all.'

Nic smiled. 'Another three down, and now we're off to court.'

23

A few hours later, Nic, Rose and Polly were in the courtroom waiting for proceedings to commence and sitting directly behind the prosecution desk. The bailiff nodded to the gathered few: 'All rise. Judge Chris Compton residing.'

The judge came from his antechamber, sat down, thumped his gavel a few times to get everyone's attention, then addressed the lawyers: 'This is for a plea only. I don't want any theatrics from anybody in my courtroom. Is your client ready to make a plea, Ms Scarlett?' The Defence Attorney nodded and the Judge looked towards Scott Free, who was now standing: 'How do you plead, Mr Free?'

'Not guilty, your Honour.'

'This case involves a multitude of frauds committed against Banks and the State and involves millions of dollars. Do you have anything else to say?'

'Not guilty, Your Honour.'

'Not guilty of what, exactly?'

Scott Free looked at his attorney, then at the judge. 'Of not being guilty.' The Judge shrugged, then hammered down the gavel. 'Bail is set at one hundred thousand dollars.' Scott Free smiled, albeit a little prematurely, then whispered to his lawyer: 'Will they take a Credit Card?' The bailiff overheard the comment and nodded to the judge, who responded with an increase in bail.

'Make it half a million dollars. I bet you can't get your hands on that much to keep you out of jail.' Scott Free smiled again and was about to respond when his lawyer slapped him over the back of the head. 'Zip it, Scott.' The judge was about to leave the room when Nic stood up. 'I'm sorry, Your Honour. May I have a quick word?' The judge looked at Nic. 'And you are?'

'Nic Thorn, from Nic Thorn and Associates, representing the interested parties.'

'Are you an attorney?'

'No, Your Honour, however, I would like a moment of your time before the defendant leaves the court.'

'It is highly unusual, but make it quick and ensure it is relevant to the case.'

Nic moved around to the bench and shook the hand of the prosecutor. 'My question is to the defence lawyer. I believe she has not fully disclosed a conflict of interest in this case.'

The judge lowered his glasses, rubbed his eyes, and looked down at the lawyer. 'Ms. Scarlett, is there something you have not divulged to my court?'

'No, Your Honour.'

Nic sighed. 'I think Ms Scarlett needs to be honest with the court.'

The lawyer glared at Nic, raised her briefcase from the floor and held it against her chest. 'Your Honour, I cannot divulge the truth now.' The judge was standing up with gavel in hand to demand an explanation. 'Stop with the theatrics. You have appeared in my court previously, and you know I don't suffer fools gladly. You either detail the matter, or I will hold you in contempt, and you know how much paperwork that means for me.'

Scott Free swapped positions with his lawyer, and made his way closer to the exit, then forcefully pushed her sideways, causing her to topple to the floor. He then leaped over the little brown door separating the gallery from the legal sanctum and the gathered few watched as he escaped through the rear doors. The bailiff had been distracted by the judge and was not ready for the interruption.

Rose called out. 'Do you want to go after him, Nic?'

'Nup. He's got nowhere to go. Ms Scarlett, however, might be spending tonight at his majesties pleasure.'

The judge banged his gavel onto the desk. 'Bailiff, please lead Ms Scarlett into my chamber. You, Mr Thorn, you come too. I want to know what this is all about. Bring the others too.'

Nic leaned towards Rose and Polly. 'I'll catch you later at the airport.'

The group was led into the judge's chamber, and he sat behind the desk. 'Mr Thorn, why have you interrupted my day? I was looking forward to an early lunch.' Nic nodded. 'I'm sorry, Your Honour; however, this matter has been developing for quite some time, and I have it on good advice that neither of them intended to re-appear in your court after today's hearing.'

The judge looked at the attorney. 'Is that correct, Ms Scarlett?'

Ms Scarlett smiled. 'Well, it's not every day that you get one up on the banks.'

The judge clasped his fingers and shook his head. 'So you are involved in the perpetration of the fraud?'

'Not guilty, Your Honour, and if there is nothing else for us to discuss, may I formally request that I leave your court.' The lawyer looked around and turned to make her departure. 'Well, at least from your little chamber anyway.'

Nic raised his hand. 'Your Honour, there is a little matter of contempt. That might hold her a little longer.'

The judge waived his hand down and glared at the woman. 'Ms Scarlett, I hereby sentence you to four hours. Bailiff, please lead Ms Scarlett to the cell.'

'Sorry, Your Honour, but you may not want to do that.' The judge re-directed his gaze towards the Bailiff, who was now leading the attorney towards the door. 'But why are you deciding what I should be doing?' The Bailiff grinned. 'Because she's not guilty, and neither am I, of anything.'

The duo then left the chamber and slammed the door behind them.

The judge stood up, and Nic took a step towards him. 'I'm sorry, Your Honour, my investigations didn't make any further connection between Ms Scarlett, Mr Free, and your bailiff. We missed something.'

The judge nodded. 'So did I. Never mind, they shouldn't get far.'

Nic moved towards the window and called the judge over, and they watched as the trio stepped into a black limousine and drive away. The judge shook his head. 'Now, that does mean paperwork. I'll make a call and get a BOLO on them.' Nic stepped back to the desk. 'No need, Your Honour. The driver is one of mine.' He lay his phone face up and pressed the speaker so they could overhear the conversation from the car.... *That judge is a knob.*

I've been working with him for weeks, and he never once asked me my name or anything about me.'

Scott responded: 'Which is a good thing, Barton, as the less he knows about you, the harder you'll be to find.' The bailiff nodded. 'I never thought of it that way.'

The driver interrupted them. 'Where are we off to?'

'Just drive to the airport. We'll be stopping at the Australia Post storage boxes outside the shopping centre,. Then you can drive us to the terminal. Don't do anything stupid, driver, and put up the privacy screen.'

The driver nodded, and the screen rose. Ms Scarlett opened her briefcase and handed the travel arrangements to the others. 'We're on separate flights. Scott, yours leaves in an hour to Singapore, Barton, you're off to Fiji at three, and I'm heading to the Sunshine Coast Airport on a domestic QANTAS flight, then onto New Zealand.'

She then handed each of them a Nokia mobile phone. 'Remember that these are for text use only; do not make any calls, even to say goodbye to anyone. We've got to get out of Australia. I assume that you've read the updated plan?' Both Scott and Barton nodded, and then he smiled. 'I didn't even get to say goodbye to my ex-wife. Does this mean I never have to talk to her again?'

Ms Scarlett glared at him. 'Do you still have your other phone?' He nodded. 'Give it to me.' Barton handed it over, and she removed the SIM, bent it in half, then opened the back of the phone and snapped the motherboard.

Barton smiled again. 'I definitely won't be able to call her now. What a shame.'

Nic was on a computer in the judge's chambers searching the flight details for familiar names. 'Found them. It looks like they're on different flights. We'll have to stop them after they collect whatever they have in storage, but my driver will keep tabs on them.'

'This is a big set-up, Mr Thorn. How long have you known about it?'

'At least sixteen months. They were using the property at Queanbeyan as a base to store equipment until it was sold and converted to cash. My team's investigations revealed that they transferred some of the holdings to a storage unit, but I wasn't aware that people in the legal fraternity were also involved. We can't stop them until they break the law, and at this stage, we don't exactly know what they are collecting.'

'Who brought you in?'

'Both banks and the AFSA. They'd noticed some anomalies with data on their PPSR system and contacted me to look.'

'That's interesting, as I would have thought they have their investigators.'

'They do, but they outsourced it once it exceeded their scope. In this case, it appears that there were wheels within wheels.'

'Did you have to do much chasing?'

'I did broker the purchase of the neighbouring property to keep an eye on things, and it went from there. We got a bit lucky, though, as one of my team members overheard a couple of men discussing the matter. Did you hear about that crash the other day where a forklift fell off a truck?'

The judge nodded. 'It delayed traffic for hours.'

'They were part of their team, too.'

'It's coming full circle then?'

'Not quite, as we've still got to stop them at the airport. I may have used up all my favours the time I stopped Scott Free from flying away. I'll have to think of something else.'

'Please let me know if you need any help. I've got a few contacts around the place.' The judge stood up to shake Nic's hand. 'Thorn, you said your name was Nic Thorn. I know a Thorn that works for ....'

Nic raised his hand. 'It's likely to be my Father, but he prefers not to let anyone know who he works for. Not even me.'

24

Around an hour later, the driver was parked inside the airport precinct, waiting in a no-standing zone at the shopping centre adjacent to the airport entrance. The trio had stepped out, each carrying a large shopping bag. The bags appeared to be full of clothing.

An Airport Security Officer approached the car, the driver became concerned that her passengers would miss their flights. He rapped on the window. 'Lower the window, please.' The driver nodded.

'You are not permitted to wait here without a permit. It is a secured area.'

'Sorry, Officer, but I'm waiting for my passengers. They're collecting luggage from the Australia Post storage site by the shopping centre's entrance. I believe they will only be a few more minutes.'

The Officer nodded. 'If I return from my rounds and see you here waiting, I will be very cranky.'

The driver looked for the name badge and noticed it was upside down. 'Sure. Officer...are you with me ...us?'

"I'm not sure what you mean, young lady; however, please ensure your passengers make their flights, but don't be alarmed if they get stopped along the way and your vehicle is searched.'

The driver nodded and smiled.

Meanwhile, standing by the storage unit, the two men had removed the contents of the bags and donned full-length puffer jackets. Each had been modified with additional internal pockets. They shielded each other and stuffed their pockets with the bundles of cash. Ms Scarlett had returned from the centre's toilets having donned a 'pregnancy suit' and was happy with the result; as she filled her suit, Scott grinned at her. 'Have you got a spare?'

'You're an idiot. You should have moved some of this the other day, but you made me alter the plan.'

Scott grimaced. 'You know that a Flight Marshall boarded the plane, and I had to make a getaway. I jumped off but got caught. I still don't know who paid for the seat upgrade. Did you do that?'

Ms Scarlett grumbled. 'Nope, you idiot. Did it occur to you that they are on to us, and that was just a ploy to stop you from leaving Australia?'

'I suppose it could have been. Why do you think they are onto us?'

'Well, for a start, you were stopped from making a getaway, and secondly, the others have already been taken into custody. Thirdly, the Police have seized the unsold equipment.'

Scott continued: 'We were careful, although the neighbour was a little nosy. I think we eventually scared him off. I heard they took a pot-shot at his dog.'

Ms Scarlett shook her head. 'Did you bother to ask him why he was being nosy, as that might have been an opportunity to establish some rapport? Anyway, I found out that the property next door changed hands earlier this year, and he didn't look like the sort of guy that could come up with a couple of million bucks to buy it, did he?'

Scott nodded. 'The only thing I noticed about him was that he had one leg.'

'You're such an idiot, and I can't believe we've gotten this far. We are so close to the end. Let's get the last of these bundles hidden so we can get out of here.' Ms Scarlett opened her briefcase and extracted two AUSTRAC forms. 'Sign these forms. They declare you are taking over ten thousand dollars out of Australia. They will check it, too, so have the cash ready. The forms show that you recently sold some mining equipment and have the invoices to confirm. Also, tell them you recently sold your computer, so you had to complete the paper form rather than online.'

Barton nodded. 'You've got this all sorted, haven't you?'

'Almost. The next bit will be the hardest as we leave Australia, and people may try to stop us.' The driver had given up waiting for them to return, left the car and approached them. 'Are you ready yet? I've already been told to move the car.' The group turned and followed the driver back to the vehicle. Barton and Scott tried to shield their colleague, but the driver happened to notice her sudden weight gain in the last fifteen minutes. 'Sorry, I didn't realise you were heavily pregnant.'

The trio then climbed into the car for the short drive to the airport terminal.

In the meantime, Nic had relocated to the Airport Security Monitoring Office and watched the car on the television screens. The Supervisor nodded at the moving vehicle. 'I assume the driver won't move to delay them?'

'Nope, she won't, so we have to stop them just before they board. Do you have anything in mind?' The man nodded. 'I'll get the system to flag the ticket when they're at the boarding gate, so that might slow them down.'

Nic smiled. 'How about they are announced as the winners of a major bonus Frequent Flyer point competition? That shouldn't raise any suspicions when they are stopped. We'll see how it goes.'

The trio were dropped off, and they had only carry-on suitcases trailing behind them as they headed into the airport concourse. Barton and Scott had been reminded to be upfront about declaring their cash holdings, albeit much less than they were carrying. Ms Scarlett had also timed their approach to coincide with another of her team members who would be conducting the wand search. She knew she would be directed to a separate aisle due to her pregnancy, and he would collect the AUSTRAC declarations. When they moved to the front of the security queue, the attendant nodded at her pregnancy and directed Ms Scarlett towards the person holding the wand.

Scott tapped at this chest. 'I've got a pacemaker, ' Barton said, tapping his hips and knees. 'Metal hip. I'm like The Terminator. All metal.' The attendant also pointed them to the Security Officer holding the wand. There were no delays, and the trio cleared the security checkpoint, entered the shopping precinct, and went their separate ways.

Back in the AMSO, the Supervisor had watched the process unfold and shook his head in dismay. 'That's why we've introduced the full body scanners. It should be impossible to hide anything now. I'll also arrange a review of our wand protocols as that was too easy for them.'

Nic nodded. 'There must be more cash stashed somewhere in the airport. They would only be carrying about fifty thousand each, but the scam made them nearly double that. I'll get my team to follow them, too.' Nic tapped at his ear. 'Polly, Rose...you're up. Don't get too close; you know the drill.'

The Supervisor switched the screens to follow them individually, and he tapped his finger on the suitcases. 'The security scanners didn't show anything other than clothes in their cases.'

They kept watching and realised the men were approaching a toilet alcove. An A-frame board was across the entry: 'Closed for Cleaning.' The men ignored the sign and entered the toilets.

Over in the airport shopping area, Rose was watching Ms Scarlett shuffle down the corridor; she too was approaching a toilet corridor. It also had a 'Closed for Cleaning' sign across the open space. Rose took a photo of the woman and found a seat at the City Hill Coffee outlet to wait to see what was to happen next. The woman didn't take long and returned to the general-purpose area in a few minutes. Rose again took a picture with her phone, studied the two images, and then watched the woman head to her gate. Rose emailed Nic the photographs and then phoned him. 'She swapped the cases.'

Nic held the first image against the screen they were watching, and the Supervisor checked it. 'I can't see any difference.'

Nic muttered. 'Good pick up, Rose.' Nic leaned forward and tapped the pause button on the monitor, then held his phone against it.

'The name label has changed positions. It was on the side before she went in, and now it's on the handle of the prongs. She changed cases or shifted the label, so I would suggest Rose is correct. Let's watch the vision of Barton and Scott.'

The supervisor switched the vision over to the men, but they didn't notice any difference between when they had entered the ablution area and when they exited.

Nic phoned Polly. 'We can see you on the camera. Can you get closer to Barton and check out his luggage.'

'What do you want me to do?'

'Try to take it off from him. Go to the Airport Travel Store and purchase a black suitcase similar to the one he is using. It's only twenty minutes before he needs to go to the gate, so we'll watch him from here. Just be ready for anything when he realises it's gone missing.'

They watched Polly enter a store, purchase the suitcase, and directed her to where Barton was now. He had made himself comfortable at the Airport bar. Polly sat beside him and initiated a conversation while she put her suitcase directly beside his. 'Hey, that looks like a nice beer. Coopers, from South Australia, you know.'

Barton ignored her as he was engrossed in the Rugby game on the large television screen, so she tried a different tack: 'Sorry, I'm a nervous flyer, and it's my first flight to Fiji. Is that where you're headed?' He sipped his beer and muttered without diverting his eyes from the game. 'I'm going nowhere, so shut up and leave me alone.'

Polly leaned back. 'Sorry, I'm only trying to make conversation. I'll leave you alone.' Polly then stood up and bent down to pick up his case. Barton hadn't noticed, and she quietly left the area. Up in the AMSO, Nic watched it all unfold on the screens: 'Polly, what a cracker.'

The game ended with a cheer from around the bar, and Barton called the attendant over to settle the bill. He handed him a hundred dollars and grinned. 'Keep the change. I'm out of here...permanently.' He leaned down to gather the suitcase and immediately realised it was much lighter than expected. 'What the? ...Where's that dumb woman? She's taken my case. Help, help, someone has stolen my suitcase. Security, I need security.'

Nic smiled at his response. 'I bet you don't,' Nic said, watching as several security officers approached him. The lead Officer looked at Barton: 'Please come with us, Sir.'

Over at another departure gate where Scott Free was waiting, he noticed that Barton had rushed from the bar only to be approached by security staff. He couldn't determine what was happening, so he ignored it, but then he heard a phone ringing and realised it was coming from his suitcase. He tried to forget that, too. The phone kept ringing, and as Scott knew the phone was in the top half of the bag, he carefully unclipped the lock and reached inside. 'Hello...'

'Why did you answer the phone?' It was Ms Scarlett. Scott whispered into the phone. 'Why did you ring me?'

'I saw the commotion with Barton. He's lost his suitcase.'

Scott grunted. 'Too bad. If he can't look after it, too bad, that's his problem.'

'That's not what I'm worried about, I think they're onto us already. Be careful.'

Scott shook his head. 'I'm about to board, so I'm hanging up. Goodbye, good luck and don't ever call me again. Stick to the plan, you idiot.' He smiled smugly, hung up and dropped the phone into the nearest bin. Scott then joined the queue to board the plane, and he ignored the crowd of flight attendants gathering around. As the attendant placed his boarding pass on the glass machine, it started flashing and everyone cheered: 'Congratulations, Mr Free, you are our one-millionth customer and have won a million frequent flyer points with our airline. Where would you like to go?' The gathered crowd moved forward and continued the applause.

Scott shrugged. 'I just want to board the plane, thank you.'

A man then stepped forward, holding his hands out to shake them. 'We can't let you do that, Mr Free. My name is Nic Thorn. Please come with me.' Nic clasped handcuffs over his wrists. 'It's over, Scott.' Scott looked around and realised he wasn't going to make his flight.

Meantime, Rose was in the domestic lounge watching Ms Scarlett, who had just made a phone call and was miffed with the response as she dropped her phone onto the floor and stomped on it. The flight was called, and Rose wondered how she would stop her from getting aboard. The passengers queued and were checked off, and Rose watched Ms Scarlett move along the gangway.

Unsure of what other plans Nic had in mind, Rose approached the flight attendant manning the desk. 'I'm sorry. Is there a chance I can get on this flight? I need to get to Maroochydore for a wedding. I'm sorry, I hope you've got a spare seat.'

The attendant looked at her. 'There is an envelope here for a Rose Garden. We laughed when we said the name. Are you Rose Garden?' Rose nodded. 'Yes, I am. It's an in-joke with my new husband, Dr Graham Garden. I'm refusing to change my name, and you can understand why, can't you.'

The attendant nodded and handed over the envelope. Rose ripped it open, and it contained a ticket for the flight to Maroochydore. 'Looks like he managed to get me on the flight.'

'Do you have any luggage?'

'Nope.'

'Welcome aboard then.' Rose boarded the plane and took a mental note of where Ms Scarlett was sitting as she walked along the aisle.

Rose sat and immediately texted Nic: 'On board. What now?'

It came back with: 'Enjoy the flight. Driver waiting. Follow her.' Rose settled into her seat, watched the stewards run through the safety processes, and then the captain made his announcement:

'This is your Captain Phil Goldberg speaking, and I have Co-Captain Stephanie Winton with me on the flight deck. The temperature here is around eleven degrees, but it's a balmy twenty-five at Sunshine Coast Airport. The flight is just over an hour and a half, so sit back and enjoy. To infinity and beyond.' Rose smiled in the comfort that she knew the captain was another of Nic's cohorts, and he could help out if she needed any help.

25

About an hour into the flight, Rose overheard a heated argument with the man sitting in the aisle seat opposite Ms Scarlett. 'Your phone must be in flight mode while we're in the air. Turn it off, or I'll take it off you.'

Ms Scarlett ignored his request, so the man leaned over and took the phone from her ear. 'I told you so.' The man held the phone to his ear and told the caller he would be hanging up. Ms Scarlett glared at him, retrieved the phone, and stomped towards the toilets. He called out. 'You can't make phone calls in the toilet either. Do you want to be known as the woman that crashed the plane? I don't think we care if you are on the phone with your OBGYN either.'

Ms Scarlett turned back, leaned towards him, and thrust a wad of cash into his hand. 'Shut up.' The man counted out a thousand dollars and stopped talking.

Rose wondered if it was worth getting involved, but then one of the stewards approached Ms Scarlett. 'Hand it over. I will return it to you when we land.'

Ms Scarlett glared at the man, handed the phone over and returned to her seat.

Twenty minutes later, the plane taxied to the designated area on the tarmac, and they disembarked. Rose stayed well behind the crowd to ensure she was always out of view. Ms Scarlett didn't stop to collect anything from the luggage carousel and went straight to the exit. Rose followed her into the Sunshine Coast Airport sunshine, and she'd been collected in a white Toyota Land Cruiser. Whoever was driving leaned over, and they embraced. Rose looked around for her driver when a black Tesla3 appeared beside her. The window lowered, and the driver called out. 'Get in.' It was Nic.

Rose stepped in. 'How did you beat us here? Were you on the same flight? Why did I need to fly then?'

'Boy, you ask a lot of questions.' Rose softly punched him in the arm.

'I flew up in Skyvan SC7. It took me just over half an hour. I know you don't like to fly in little planes, so I didn't want to bother you. It keeps my flying hours up.' 'Damn you, Nic. How do you get to fly all the time anyway?'

'Relocation flights. In this case, there's more demand for skydiving on the Sunshine Coast during winter than in Canberra. You'd have to dive through all the snowflakes.' Rose grinned. 'Where are we going from here?'

'That I don't know, but she is booked on a flight to New Zealand in three days. I don't know where she'll be while she's waiting, and I hope you've brought some luggage in case we have to stop over, too.'

Rose looked at him. 'You know I didn't.'

Nic smiled. 'That's OK, I packed it for you. It's in the frunk.'

'Frunk? What's a frunk?'

'These Teslas don't have an engine, so the front of the car is called the front trunk, or the frunk.' Nic pointed to a button on the display screen. 'See.'

Rose was about to respond when she saw the Land Cruiser move from the curb. 'She's on the move, Frunken-stein.' Nic waited and then followed them a few moments later. They drove down Airport Road and turned left onto David Low Way. Nic nodded. 'That's good, as it means they're not heading to Maroochydore.'

'Why is that good?'

'Overnight accommodation is too expensive down that way. Hopefully, they're heading somewhere nice like the French Quarter, Noosa, or the

Novotel at Twin Waters.' Nic continued to follow the Cruiser, staying well behind, but they didn't have to go very far as upon leaving the airport the Cruiser they turned left into the Marcoola Airport Motel and stopped in the carpark.

Nic sighed. 'Not quite what I was expecting.'

'Why?

'You can get a room here for under two hundred dollars.'

'That's a problem why?'

'No reason, it's just not what I was expecting someone carrying over two hundred thousand dollars cash would stay at.' Nic drove the car past the Hotel, parked in an off-street space, and the vehicle turned itself off. 'Would you mind seeing if they've got a room for us too?'

'For how long?'

'Make it three days at least. See if they'll take cash, as I don't want any trace of the expense. This place is a little downmarket for Nic Thorn and Associates.' Rose stepped from the car, hesitated, and came back. 'You're kidding, aren't you? I'll use the Business Card instead.' Rose went to enter the reception area but noticed Ms Scarlett was still going through the booking process, so she quickly stepped back out but could still overhear the conversation.

Ms Scarlett was folding out hundred-dollar bills: 'I know you want a credit card, but how much cash do I need to hand over for this not to happen? I'll pay whatever you want. We need to stay three nights. Here's two thousand dollars. Find us some things to do while we here.'

The young receptionist squirmed. 'I'll have to get my Dad.'

'You do that, but in the meantime, hand me a room key.'

The woman with Ms Scarlett leaned over the counter and took a key. 'We're staying in Number Five when you know.'

The couple turned and left the office.

Rose stepped into an alcove to let them by, waited, went into the reception area and then returned to the car. Nic put down his phone. 'I hope you don't want me to stay here. I just googled the place across the road. It's five stars. We can get a three-bedroom apartment for under four hundred dollars a night.'

'Sounds like a plan, but I don't think we'll spend much time there.'

'Why?'

'Because I think that Ms Scarlett and her beau will do as much as possible on the Sunshine Coast before leaving Australia.'

Rose handed over some brochures she'd collected at the reception office and fanned them on her lap. 'I would say they'll be whale watching, scuba diving, hot air ballooning and maybe even do an Everglades tour or two.'

'How do you know all of that?'

'The receptionist is booking it all. I'll go back to see her success with joining the groups at such short notice.' Rose stepped out of the car. 'Oh, and I'm happy with staying across the road, but please make it one apartment each, and I'd like a beach view, too; after all, you made me fly up from Canberra on my own. You know I don't like flying.'

'I thought it was just the little planes I fly.'

'Just the thought of flying back with you in a little plane makes me anxious.' Rose shut the car door just as Nic called out. 'But I expect we'll be driving back home to Brisbane from here...'

After about fifteen minutes, Rose returned from the office and sat back in the car. 'The poor girl was in such a tizzy as she couldn't find anything for them to do as everything was booked out. I told her to keep the money and write down on a piece of paper all the things she managed to book for them.'

'I thought you said she couldn't find anything?'

'I did, and I left your phone number as the contact when they want to be collected to be driven to the events. Tomorrow, they are going whale watching at four in the morning.'

'I'll be up early anyway for a run along the beach looking for turtles.'

They were still sitting in the car when the two women strolled past them. Nic slumped down into his seat, and Rose stayed sitting upright. 'Do you think they know they are being watched?'

'I don't know, but I don't know what they know, so we should know that they know.' Rose shook her head. 'Do you practice those idioms?'

Nic decided to leave the car and follow the women. 'Are you coming?'

Rose remained seated. 'I think we could wait a bit to see where they go. Marcoola is not a big town, with shops only on this side of the road. If they don't return in ten minutes, they've stopped for coffee somewhere.'

Nic returned to the car and sat down. 'There is the Cuba St. Coffee at the end of the shopping strip. I assume they'll head there.'

'Why?'

'They have a brochure, so they must be good, and it's named after Cuba St in Wellington, New Zealand. They're about to fly there.' Nic pulled the pamphlet from the pile and showed it to Rose. 'It also says they've got the best coffee on the Sunshine Coast.' Rose sighed and stepped out of the car. 'Let's go for a walk.'

Nic and Rose strolled down the street looking for the two women and finally reached Cuba St. Coffee, where the women sat outside in the sunshine. 'OK, we found them. Wander over there to see if you can find out what they are doing next.' Rose headed off and returned with two coffees after ten minutes. 'They told the staff in the shop they're flying to New Zealand today, not in three days.'

Nic nodded. 'They might have just said that to get their coffee quicker.'

'Nope, the waitress said they were asking her about Auckland and whether it was expensive to live there. They'd asked her where her accent was from. People from over the ditch pronounce fush and chups, not fish and chips...that sort of thing.'

Nic was about to respond when he saw the two women rise from the seats and head back their way. 'Quick, hug me or something.'

Rose looked at him. 'How about we move into the service station instead.'

Nic nodded. 'That will work.'

They followed the women back to the Marcoola Hotel and waited until they returned to the reception office. Her friend entered the Cruiser a few minutes later, and then Ms Scarlett joined her. The duo drove away, turning right onto the highway and heading back to the airport.

Rose decided to check on the receptionist to see if something had gone awry with the visit from the couple. The young woman was crying.

Rose waited for her to stop. 'Are you OK?

'I'll be OK. I told them I'd made all the bookings as you said, but they didn't believe me. I even showed them the list.'

'What happened?

'They took all the cash back and said they'd changed their plans. They're not staying and are leaving for New Zealand in two hours. They managed to change their flights. I wasn't going to argue with them. I think one of them had a gun.'

'I'm so sorry.'

'Who were they?'

'Fugitives from Canberra, but don't tell anyone just yet.'

'What did they do, rob a bank or something? They had a lot of cash.'

'No, nothing like that. They are just a couple of scammers trying to leave Australia before the whole thing crashes down around them. We've ....' Rose stopped talking as she realised the less the young woman knew, the less she would be in danger if the couple returned.

'Call your Father; maybe he'll give you the day off to go surfing.' Rose then handed over three hundred dollars cash. 'Please take this for your trouble. If they return, don't mention that I was here or that you know anything about them.' Rose left the office, returned to the car, and Nic lowered the window. 'That took a bit longer than I thought. What happened?'

'They took back all the cash from the reception-ist and told her they're not staying, but she con-firmed they're off to New Zealand today. I gave her three hundred dollars to buy a surfboard for all the trouble I caused.'

'How do you know she surfs?'

'This is the Sunshine Coast; everybody surfs.'

26

Nic parked the Tesla in the airport precinct, and they watched the couple remove suitcases from the Cruiser. Ms Scarlett sloughed the pregnancy suit and folded it into a second black carry-on suitcase. The second woman locked the Cruiser and threw the keys into a nearby bush. Rose smiled. 'I guess they're travelling light.'

Nic nodded. 'I guess that means she's going too.'

'Or, she's not going and has another car stashed somewhere, one that doesn't have any fingerprints, or they're leaving everything behind and starting anew.'

'You're getting good at this secret squirrel stuff, right?'

'Yes, learning from the best....Detective Inspector Google.'

Nic grinned. 'I guess we're headed to New Zealand. We might be able to catch up with some of your mother's cousins.'

'I can't wait.'

Nic checked the flight details and showed Rose. 'It's about an hour before they fly, so we can sit in the car or go sightseeing. Which would you prefer?'

'We're not going to try and stop them from getting on the plane?'

'Nope. I'll leave that for the Fraud Squad. Here they come now.'

A smartly dressed couple approached the car, and Nic stepped out. 'Thanks for coming, and sorry about the confusion. Our intel had them booked in three days, but they've managed to change their flights.'

'No harm done. We spent the morning at Coolum catching a few waves.'

Rose smiled. 'So you both live on the Sunny Coast, then?'

They both nodded. 'Leaving the dream.' The senior Detective ran through the plan. 'We'll approach them in the departure foyer and ask to see their VISAs.'

Rose shook her head. 'Australians don't need a VISA to travel to New Zealand.'

'Well, the Australian Government is always changing the requirements for overseas travellers, especially those involved in a major fraud. We think it's valid to detain them if their paperwork is not in order.'

The Officers gave a mock salute to Nic and headed off to the airport complex.

Rose was leaning against the car. 'So, are we driving back to Brisbane now?'

Nic shook his head. 'Not quite; I've got some paperwork to complete from the flight I took from Canberra. It will only take a couple of minutes. The plane is parked on the tarmac by the Aero School. We can walk from here.'

Nic and Rose were walking along the road adjacent to the airport doors, and Rose couldn't help but enter the foyer to see if Ms Scarlett and her friend had been apprehended. The couple were now standing at the oversized luggage counter. Rose saw a lot of grinning and nodding, then noticed as Ms Scarlett handed over a bundle of cash.

The Detectives then approached the couple, and Ms Scarlett started yelling at the Officer regarding the change in VISA requirements. 'This is absolute crap. There is no such thing as needing a VISA to fly to New Zealand. Everyone knows that. You're making it up.'

The Officer was very patient with her. 'I'm sorry, Madam, but it's only a recent policy change. I'm sure we can sort it out. Please come with us.'

The Detective put her hand on her shoulder, and Ms Scarlett brushed it away. Meanwhile, her friend was glaring at them with mouth agape.

Nic stepped up to Rose, and they both moved inside to watch the unfolding drama.

Ms Scarlett looked around, considering her options, when she saw Nic and Rose in the doorway. 'You, it's you two. This is a scam. There is no such thing as a VISA for New Zealand.'

Ms Scarlett then swung her suitcase at the head of the Detective, it connected, and she went down heavily. Her accomplice then pulled a handgun on the second Detective. 'We're leaving, and don't follow us.'

It was bedlam in the small airport foyer. People were screaming and running for the nearest exits, and Nic and Rose were pushed outside with the throng of people. They stepped aside and allowed the panicked crowd to disburse.

Rose sighed. 'That wasn't exactly how I thought it would go down. Did you see where they went?'

'Nope, but they shouldn't get far. It's only a small airport. Let's leave it to the professionals. I'll get this paperwork done so we can go home.'

Rose and Nic continued to the next hangar, albeit quicker and wary of the couple that had just absconded. Nic left Rose waiting by the flight office and approached the plane, only to be interrupted by Ms Scarlett.

Her accomplice pointed the gun at him. 'You've stuffed everything up. Get in the plane; you're flying us out of here.' Nic lowered the door, and Ms Scarlett ascended the steps, dragging the two suitcases on board.

Nic knew Rose was waiting by the Aero club and wouldn't have seen them, so he called her on the phone. 'Rose, it looks like I'm going flying. Call Chewy to access the Tesla, and drive home to Brisbane. Meantime, hide.'

The accomplice snatched the phone from him and stomped on it. 'Who did you call? I assume it wasn't the Police as they already know where somewhere.'

Nic nodded. 'I called my friend and told her I'm taking you both on a joy flight.'

'Where is she?'

'As of right now... I have no idea, and that's the honest truth.'

Ms Scarlett looked at Nic suspiciously. 'I doubt that. Anyway, I don't care, get on the plane.' Her accomplice handed her the gun, and she pointed it at Nic. 'I know you flew up here in this plane, so now you can fly us out of here.'

Nic sighed, stepped into the pilot's chair, and donned the headphones. Ms Scarlett sat beside him while her accomplice secured the door and buckled herself into the nearest seat. "This is Romeo Delta One-Seven-One. Looking for clearance to fly. I have two passengers needing to escape the airport immediately."

"Roger, Romeo Delta One-Seven-One. We have notified all planes into holding patterns until you have departed."

Nic looked over to Ms Scarlett. 'We need to advise a course and manifest.'

She shook her head. 'No, you don't. Get moving.'

Nic taxied the Skyvan SC7 to the runway, and a couple of minutes later, they were airborne, heading east over Mudjimba Island. 'It's only water out this way until Hawaii, and I don't have enough fuel for that, so where am I headed?'

'North, Mr Thorn, North.'

Nic steered the plane north, and he flew along the coast towards Noosa.

Ms Scarlett rose from the co-pilot seat, moved into the aisle, and sat down. 'I'm so sorry, Gertie. It wasn't supposed to be this hard. I thought it was a good plan until these guys got involved.'

'Who are they?'

'I have no idea, but they seem to know much about the scam I put together.'

'Do you think you'll still get away with it?' Ms Scarlett smiled. 'They haven't caught us yet, and have no idea where we're heading.'

'Do you?'

'Yes, I'll get him to head northwest in a minute or so. I've got a landing organised at Barcaldine, and we'll hide out there for a while until things quieten down.'

'How will you convince the pilot to land the plane?'

'I'm not. He's going to jump out, and I'll land it. I'm sure they'll guide us down when we need to. You hear of emergency landings all the time.'

'I'm not sure if I want to throw him out....that's murder.'

'I'll give him a parachute. They'll be stored in the back somewhere as they use this type of plane for skydiving. Go and find one for him.' Gertie got up and went further into the plane. 'Found them. How many do you want?'

'Leave them there. I'll get him to select his own, so he can't say we're trying to fool him.' Ms Scarlett moved into the cockpit and tapped Nic on the shoulder. 'Put it on auto and get a parachute.'

Nic pressed 'Auto' and stood. 'This isn't my plane, so please take care of it.'

Ms Scarlett jabbed him in the ribs. 'Don't get smart with me, fly-boy.' Nic selected a parachute, then took another and held it up. 'I assume you wanted two?' He placed them down on the floor next to the black suitcases. 'How long until you make the jump?'

'When we get over Carnarvon National Park, not long.'

Nic returned to the pilot seat, but Ms Scarlett told him to sit on the other side. 'I'll be taking it from here, and you'll be making the jump, not us.'

Nic nodded and realised they were nearing the drop zone. 'Do you know how to fly this plane or even land it? Flying is easy; landing is hard.'

'Not your problem. Now move to the rear and raise the rear ramp.'

Nic pressed the lever to open the plane's rear, stood up and shuffled along the aisle. He donned the parachute, but not before stopping to conspicuously tie his boot laces and secretly loop a rope around the second parachute and the handles of the suitcases. He then secured the end to his waist. Nic moved towards the opened rear ramp, turned to face them, saluted, and then fell backward into the void. Ms Scarlett and Gertie watched him; then they noticed a rope becoming taut along the floor. It was taking the second parachute. 'I guess he didn't trust us,' then they watched as the suitcases were dragged along and dropped overboard.

Gertie rushed to the open end of the plane and looked down to see that Nic had deployed his parachute. She released her grip on the guide rope, took a shooting stance, and pointed the gun into the sky below, trying to aim. The plane wobbled, so having to prioritise her safety, she angrily threw the weapon into the blue sky. 'Oops, I shouldn't have done that. Never mind, it was a replica anyway.'

Ms. Scarlett then moved back into the cockpit, wondering if she could turn the plane around.

However, she soon realised that wasn't her primary concern as she noticed the plane was losing altitude. Gertie joined her and sat in the co-pilot seat. 'How long before we land?'

'I have no idea. I don't even know how to use the radio.'

Gertie looked around the space and then felt under the seat. 'At least we have flight instructions.' She leafed through the book and threw it behind her. 'Next step, I guess, is calling a Mayday.'

Ms Scarlett looked at her. 'I just hope my phone works from up here.' She tapped her phone, and it read: '*No Service. Emergency Use Only,*' and held it up for Gertie to see. 'We could try to ring triple zero, but that will involve the Police, so grab the book and see if it shows you how to use the radio. We need to land this thing.'

Gertie picked up the book, found the chapter on the radio, and they decided to make the call: "Mayday, Mayday. This is Romeo Delta One-Seven-One. Mayday. Mayday. Is there anyone there?"

There was no response. 'Did you put the radio on?'

'Yes. Stop yelling. If we crash, we both die.'

Gertie tried again, but this time, the radio crackled with a response: "*Roger, Romeo Delta One-Seven-One. We acknowledge your Mayday. What is your emergency?*"

Gertie pushed the button again. 'Listen. We've lost our pilot and are going down.'

"We have you on tracking at four thousand feet, currently flying above Mexico."

Gertie responded angrily: 'We're in Australia, you dumb ass.'

There was no response, so Ms Scarlett took control of the radio. 'We are losing altitude and were expecting to land at Barcaldine. Will we make it?'

"Roger. Mexico is approximately eighty kilometres from Barcaldine. We will assist you in landing at Barcaldine Airport. Have you flown a plane before?"

Ms Scarlett responded: 'No, but I've heard this plane is easy to fly but hard to land.'

"Roger that. I'll call you back with the landing process when you get closer. Ensure the auto is on so you will stay in the air."

Gertie responded: 'The red light shows that it's on.'

Meantime, about a hundred kilometres away, Nic was folding up his parachute, wondering where he'd landed, but at least it was close to a homestead. Both suitcases had survived the fall, and he was busy rolling through the combinations trying to open them when a farmer approached him riding on a tractor. The farmer stopped and climbed off. 'That was quite a fall. The only jumpers we normally get around here are the kangaroos.'

The case suddenly snapped open, and the farmer peered inside at the bundles of cash. Nic grinned. 'I know, so don't jump to any conclusions about me. I'm not a bank robber. I'm working with the Fraud Squad, and we're closing in on a couple about to land their plane at Barcaldine. How quickly can you get me there?'

The farmer smiled. 'I've got a few toys around the place. It's about one hundred and twenty k's to Barky, so I could get you there in just over half an hour if you don't mind me driving. Come with me.'

Nic followed the farmer to a large woolshed, and the man slid open the giant steel doors to reveal a couple more tractors and a car resembling an autobot from the Transformers movies. 'I race this one in the Finke Desert Rally, and it needs a little run to blow out the cobwebs.' Nic looked over the beast of the car. It was almost growling at him. 'What's under the hood?'

'About six thousand cc's. It's a modified Holden Rodeo, and the top speed is around two hundred, so if you don't mind going fast, this will get you there.'

Nic smiled. 'Yep, that will do it.'

The farmer nodded. 'Now let's talk about my fee. From what I saw in that case, I'm sure you could meet the fuel cost.' Nic handed over a bundle of cash. 'I think there's about five thousand in here. It will also cover the cost of your entry fee into the race. That's about fourteen hundred last time I went.' The farmer pocketed the bundle, and Nic continued. 'Would you mind doing me a favour, though? This is not my money; will you certify an IOU?'

The farmer smiled. 'I'm the local magistrate around these traps. I can do that.' They climbed into the car, and the farmer held out his hand. 'Alen Twelftree, nice to meet you.' Nic nodded. 'Nic Thorn. I run an investigation business around Australia. My team catches scammers and fraudsters, and this is the biggest we've been involved with in a while.'

'How much is big?'

'It involved falsifying data and selling mining equipment under finance leases. Two banks were involved, a lawyer and a handful of thugs. We believe it was upwards of three quarters a million dollars.'

'And you stopped them?'

'Not without help. I've got a team of about ten, which reminds me, can I use your phone as I need to make a call.'

Twelftree nodded, handed over the phone, and started his pre-start-up routine with the car. Nic moved away to make the call, which was answered quickly: 'This is Rose.'

'Hi, Rose. I'm safe. I almost got the jump on them but had to take a leap of faith.'

Rose hesitated. 'Where are you? And what's that supposed to mean?'

'I'm about a hundred or so k's from Barcaldine, west of Rockhampton, and as for the leap of faith, they threw me out of the plane, well, I jumped.'

'Oh, my God.'

'I know, lucky I had a parachute. Besides that, I'm about to get into a modified Holden Rodeo and drive to Barky in just over half an hour.'

Rose went quiet. 'A Holden Rodeo, how? Does it drive at warp speed?'

'Almost, but no, a lovely farmer is driving me. It's his rally car and tops out at about two hundred. I'll get there just in time to help them land the plane.'

'Don't they know how to fly it?

'Fly it, probably; land it, no. They were relying on someone on the ground to guide them down. I guess that might be me.' The roar from the massive car's engine reverberated in the shed, and Nic had to yell to continue: 'That's my cue to hang up. I'll see you back in Brisbane.'

Twelftree stepped inside and buckled himself into a five-belt harness. 'I hope you don't mind me driving fast.' Nic nodded, buckled himself in and donned a crash helmet. 'As long as we get there in one piece.'

The car took off, and the acceleration propelled Nic back into his seat. Twelftree was in total control, even offering hand signals for the turns they took at excessive speeds. After thirty minutes, they were on the outskirts of Barcaldine. He slowed the car to a crawl. The speed limit in town is only fifty. I'm still doing ninety, so I'd better slow down.' They reached the airport, and Nic climbed out. 'Thanks for that, Alen, and good luck at Finke.' The car roared to life again, and Twelftree drove out of the airport carpark and disappeared from view. Nic could still hear the engine's throb, but he didn't know if the noise was coming from inside his head.

Nic entered the airport, asked for the Operations Manager, and was escorted to the flight tower. He shook a few hands and noticed the emergency protocols had been implemented. 'I was flying the plane, so I can guide her down if you prefer.'

The Manager looked at him. 'What happened? Why did they throw you out?'

'It's a long story, and I'm happy to explain it later, but I think we'd better focus on getting this bird down. They don't know how to fly or land it, but before I jumped out, they mentioned they were planning an Emergency landing.'

One of the controllers sheepishly put their hand up. 'I'm sorry, it was me. I happened to mention that our airport was overdue for the training exercise two weeks ago when I was sitting in a bar at the Brisbane airport. It all went from there. She paid me two thousand dollars cash to set it up.' The Operations Manager nodded. 'I guess it's your shout when all this is over.'

Nic donned the headset and called up the plane: *'Romeo Delta One-Seven-One, this is Barcaldine airport. We have implemented safety protocols and will bring you in for a landing. Please both be seated in the cockpit. I will need one person on the controls and the other to be my eyes and ears.'*

Gertie responded. 'About time.'

Nic ignored her comment. *I need you to initiate the landing sequence. Please find the fuel booster. It is left of the horizon screen. Can you see it? There is plenty of fuel.'* Ms Scarlett responded this time. 'Yes.'

'I am going to get you to switch off the auto-pilot. The plane will most likely jolt a little. Do not push or pull the yoke. Hold it lightly. Please now check the engine revs, switch on the wheel brakes and practice lowering the flaps.'

'OK.'

'The auto-pilot button is to your right. Please push it in.'

'OK....I'm flying it...I'm flying it.'

'Now push the yoke very slowly away from you. This will lower the nose.'

'OK. Yes, the plane is heading down. That was easy.'

'As I said, flying is easy; landing is hard.'

The radio suddenly went quiet: *'Are you there, Romeo Delta One-Seven-One?*

'Yes, we are. Get us down now, and I want my suitcases back.'

They landed safely and followed Nic's instructions to the letter. Nic then directed them to taxi to the side of the airport so flights could continue as normal. Once the plane had stopped, Ms Scarlett was instructed to complete the shutdown checks and turn off all systems, but she refused to disembark. It wasn't until three hours later that they decided to admit defeat, and Nic escorted the couple from the plane to the waiting Police.

Nic kept the suitcases.

27

The following afternoon, Nic stood outside Sandy's place in West End and rang the doorbell. Rose answered the door. 'So Maverick, you decided to come back.'

'Yep, flying makes me tired. Especially when you have to coach someone to land in a plane, they don't know how to fly.' Rose let him inside and nodded. 'I heard she did a good job. It made the evening news. Nothing about the scam she was involved in; they just mentioned it was an emergency landing.'

'I know, and I had to shell out some cash to keep that part out of the news.' Nic lifted a suitcase, put it on the kitchen table, and clicked it open. Rose peered inside. It was full of IOUs, no bundles of cash. 'Where is the money?'

Nic started to dance to the routine from the Jerry Maguire movie. 'Show me the money....show me the money...'

Rose looked at him. 'Stop that; you're scaring me.'

Nic kept dancing, so Rose continued talking. 'Sandy has COVID if you want to know. Her Father is still in hospital but out of ICU.' Nic stopped mid-groove. 'I'm sorry to hear that. There's talk about the states closing the borders with this thing, which might make it interesting for us to get to Kangaroo Island to watch the K.P.I. Event thing.'

'Are we still going? I thought we'd missed out on looking into that?'

'Yep, I'm planning on attending, even if it's not in an official capacity as a scam buster.' Rose shut the case and put it on the floor. 'So you think it is a scam?'

'I do, but don't tell anyone. I hoped to go to use my winnings to replace my IOUs.'

Rose put her hands on her hips. 'Where is the cash, Nic?'

'I think they call it evidence. I left it with the Police in Brisbane. They didn't need to keep this suitcase as I bought it at the airport. If cases like these can take a fall from seven thousand feet, I'm sure it can take anything I use it for.'

Rose softly punched him in the arm. 'So where to next?'

'We fly back to Canberra and finalise the purchase of the property next door to mine. Did you know that the Bank will take any reasonable offer to cover their loss when it's a mortgagee sale?'

Rose nodded. 'So you'll be the King of Queanbeyan with all the landholding.'

'You could be my Queen, Rose. The Rose Queen of Queanbeyan beats being the Tulip Queen of the Floriade. Are you interested in being a part-owner?'

Rose looked at him. 'I'm sure I could manage to ante up something. Do you have any plans for the farm? Are you going to run them both as going concerns?'

'Well, I've already lodged for subdivision approval with the local council. So, there's talk of developing both properties into low-cost housing sites. Small land allotments, that sort of thing.'

'Whose talk?'

'Mine and my Fathers.'

'Oh, so you talk to him then?'

'Nope, just through his attorney.'

'Will I get to meet him to talk things through?'

'Yes, but only through his attorney, and if he's not too busy saving the world.'

'From what?'

'I never ask him.'

Rose thought about it. 'OK. I'm in. How much do I have to put up?'

'About three hundred thousand to purchase, then a couple of hundred to get the land subdivided, roads built, services, that sort of thing.' Rose nodded. 'That's a lot of things. Have you spoken to Sandy about it?'

'Not yet, but how about we call her now and see how she is going?'

Rose dialled Sandy and put the call on speaker. 'Hey, Sandy. How is it going?'

'This thing I've got, we've got, it's a doozy. Most of the town is about to be shut down. There's talk of closing the state borders, too.'

Nic leaned forward. 'I know, I'm trying to organise flights to Adelaide before they close the borders. We should get there. The Kangaroo Island thing will probably still go ahead to a lesser extent. I want to be there to see how they manage.'

'I don't think you...We shouldn't catch up. It's pretty contagious. I suggest you get updated jabs.' Rose nodded. 'I already have. Listen, I know you probably...um... Nic has a business proposal for us about buying the land next to the farm in Canberra and subdividing it. We must put in about three hundred grand, plus other money to cover the development costs. What do you think?' Sandy coughed. 'If my Father can come in too, we can manage it.'

Rose hesitated with her response. 'How is your Father?'

'He's home with me now. It all got a bit scary, so we've set up a Power of Attorney in case something happens. I'll be able to sign for anything on his behalf. He's cashed up since he did the stint working in Antarctica and is always looking for somewhere safe to park some of his super. Land is safe. He's told me that.'

Nic leaned back. 'Can you shoot me a copy of the POA documents? I'll get my people to have a look to make sure they're all Kocher, and then we'll draw up a Partnership Agreement. I hate paper-work, so it will be low-key, based on contribution, that sort of thing.'

'OK. We've both got a couple more days in iso. It will give us something to distract us from this thing we've both got...or had. Anyway, I'll leave it to you guys to sort things out. I'm going back to bed.'

They disconnected, and Rose logged into the airline's flight site. 'There's talk here about all the state borders being closed.'

'Yep, but we are an exception. We can still travel as 'Essential Service People'.

'Why is what we do an essential service?'

'It stops people from being scammed.' Rose softly punched Nic in the arm again.

Nic then made further inquiries about the flights and realised that if they could be ready in a few hours, they could be in Adelaide by later tonight. 'Can you pack for Adelaide? There's a flight in three hours that we can catch.'

Rose nodded. 'Dog is still over at Dave's place, so I'll go over there and check if he can keep him for another week.' Rose stood up. 'Back in a tick.'

'Don't hurry, as I've got to make a few calls to get things underway.'

Rose met with Dave, the neighbour, in his front yard. He was trying to entice Dog, the cat, to chase a piece of rope. Dave looked up as Rose approached.

'Your cat doesn't like exercise, does he?'

'He exercises every time he eats. It's just his jaw, but it's still exercise. Anyway, are you OK with continuing to look after him? Sandy is still in Adelaide with COVID, and Nic and I are about to go down there too. There's a horse race on Kangaroo Island that he wants us to watch.'

Dave nodded. 'You guys spend a lot of time investigating stuff, don't you?'

'Yes, I guess that's what we do now. I discovered recently that one of Nic's drivers, Driver, holds a PI license. Sandy and I completed the course a couple of months ago but never thought we'd use it.'

'Should I get one too?'

'Are you going to be investigating stuff with us?'

'Nope, it's just that it would look good on my resume. Was there much study?'

'We did ours through the Private Investigators College. It took a couple of months. We didn't tell Nic we were studying it until we completed it.'

'Did he pay for it?'

'Nope, but we could claim it on tax as part of our employment.'

Dave sighed. 'Maybe I'll study something else then, like astronomy. I like watching the stars at night. Did you know they shine during the day too, but the sun is too bright.'

'I did, and thanks again, Dave. I'll see you in a couple of weeks.'

Rose returned to her place and waited for Nic to get off the phone. Rose could hear the caller was getting rather animated during the discussion, but she couldn't make out whom he was talking to. Nic eventually hung up and took a breath. 'Well, that was interesting. Anyhow, we bought the place next door to the farm.'

'OK, I'll tell Sandy to check her finances. A normal sixty-day settlement, I suspect, so we have some time.'

'Actually, don't worry about it. The subdivision proposal was declined, so we must do more work before resubmitting. We'll cover the initial purchase as it went for a lot less than we thought, and the council has told us we must wait until next year to try again.' Rose nodded. 'So why does that affect us?'

'We only paid six hundred thousand for it.'

'I thought you'd put in a pre-auction offer for almost a million?'

'We did, and that was the Real Estate Agent on the phone. He is saying that we blind-sided him, and we may be taken to court about it.'

'What did you do?'

'Well, I had Gus bid for us as our representative at the auction. One of the issues with the subdivision was road access; it would have to be through our property, so as we already owned it, it would be OK.'

'So what was the issue? The Land Agent didn't tell anyone about that?'

'He did. He rang to tell me he was sorry I didn't get the property at the auction, and wanted to know if we were interested in something else. When I told him that Gus did our bidding and that he should apologise to the seller as they missed out on another four hundred thousand, he got a little cranky and sweary.'

Rose smiled. 'Didn't you tell him that Gus was doing the bidding for you?'

'Gus tried to, but when he registered his details, they only wanted his name and address, not whom he represented. They called it an 'office error', and that's why he's cranky.' Rose smiled again. 'It sounds like it's their problem.'

'It is. Anyway, I'll get my Father's lawyer to sort it out. Meantime, we've got to get to Adelaide before they shut the borders.'

Rose nodded. 'We could get stranded in South Australia.'

'Maybe, so pack warm.'

28

Around five hours later, Nic and Rose stood outside Sandy's father's house in Rose Park. Sandy was standing behind the meshed screen door. 'I told you guys not to visit us. This thing is as catchy as The Wiggle's new song.'

Nic smiled. 'We're just passing through and saw your light on. Besides, we need access to a car, and the Hire Companies have been told not to release anything because of COVID-19. Does Robb have one we could borrow?'

Sandy moved away from the door and returned a few moments later with a keycard. 'You'll need to take the Tesla out. On one condition, though,'

'What's that? We go to Bunnings and buy a large extension cord?'

A laugh sounded from behind Sandy, then a hacking cough. It was Robb. 'Don't make me laugh. Adelaide has over fifty charging stations now.'

Sandy looked back at Nic. 'The condition is that Rose drives it out.'

Nic and Rose wheeled their luggage to the garage and raised the roller door. The car was a bright yellow Tesla Y Performance model. Nic whistled. 'Wow, I must be paying Robb too much if he can afford one of these. It's about a hundred grand's worth.'

Rose shook her head. 'He doesn't work for you. Besides, Sandy said, 'You'll have to take the Tesla out, as in shift it, so that we can get to the car behind it, not take it to KI with us.'

Nic assisted Rose in carefully moving the Tesla onto the street and returned to the garage. Another car was under a tarpaulin, and Nic peeked under the cover, then grinned. 'I think we should take the Tesla. It's worth less than this one.'

Rose sighed and helped Nic fold the cover. It revealed a 1967 Mustang Shelby. Nic whistled again. 'Left-hand drive too, so I reckon about a hundred grand.' Rose nodded. 'Yes about that, and unfortunately, you aren't licensed to drive it.'

Nic looked at her. 'I've driven lefties before.'

'Here in SA, you must be registered to drive a lefty. It's one of those state-based road rules.' Rose pulled her phone out and pressed on the mySAGOV license app. 'Like this one I have.' Nic shook his head. 'Damn you, Rose.'

Rose shook her head again. 'But we're not taking that one either. It's that one.'

Nic looked up and saw another car parked in front of the Mustang. 'How many cars does he own?'

Rose grinned. 'We own, as in Sandy and I. We don't just flip cars in Brisbane; we've done at least three since we did the Jensen Interceptor and the little Morgan that old mate partly swapped for. Adelaide has a big demand for classic cars renovated to spec, so Robb taps into the market for us. We should check out the National Motor Museum in Birdwood if we have the time.'

Nic nodded, then moved up to the next car. It was a 1972 Karmann Ghia Convertible in red. Rose patted the vehicle on the canvas roof. 'We've just finished this one. It took over a year to get all the parts from the UK, and don't worry, I'll let you drive it. The keys are in the ignition.'

After about half an hour of manoeuvring cars and carefully saying goodbye to Robb and Sandy, Rose and Nic were heading south for Cape Jervis. It was usually an hour and forty-minute drive. The car ferry departs from that point across the Backstairs Passage to Penneshaw on Kangaroo Island.

The trip took over two hours every time the dynamic duo stopped; admirers took photographs of the car. Nic ensured he wasn't caught in the frame, so Rose was the one who had to keep smiling. They left Normanville, and Rose was now driving, so Nic organised the ferry fare online.

Rose drove the car onto the ferry and pulled the vehicle to a stop. 'Where are we staying on KI?'

'Lynette's, at American River. We follow the road and take the turnoff.'

Rose stepped out of the car. 'Who is Lynette? You know I only like to stay in five-star hotels. I don't do Airbnb.'

'Not quite. You'll have to wait and see. How about we go up to the deck level and get a drink? I have to wash the bugs out of my teeth.'

Rose and Nic went upstairs and collected a paper map of Kangaroo Island from a tourist information carousel. They sat down at a table, and Rose folded it out. 'Apparently, there's not much phone coverage on the island, so old school, I'm afraid. Can you read a map?'

Nic looked at her. 'Read one, yes, need for one, no. I don't use maps. I use my intuition, raw courage, and Google.'

Rose sighed. 'I've just said there's not much phone coverage on KI, so Google Maps won't work.'

'I heard you. I hope the kangaroos can help out if we get lost. I'm confident we won't, as we'll eventually hit the water in whatever direction we go and have to turn around. It is an island, after all.'

Rose nodded. 'So is Australia, but this is a little smaller. Anyway, how far is the racecourse from Lynette's place?'

'About a ten-minute drive. The island is about a hundred and sixty km long and takes about two hours to go east/west, but it's only about forty minutes north/south. We'll be spending most of the time up this end anyway.'

The ferry docked, and Nic drove the car off, heading for American River. He turned left into American River Road and pulled the vehicle to stop outside the Mercure Kangaroo Island Lodge. 'This is Lynette's place.'

Rose stepped out of the car. 'I know this place. It used to be called Linnett's but hasn't been that for about forty years. It was once in a Pub Quiz. Jack and Valerie Linnett set up the site over a hundred years ago. It then became a Mercure and is rated four stars. I think I can cope with that.'

Nic gathered the luggage, and they went to reception. A cheerful receptionist greeted them. 'Booking for Iva and Rose Garden. You've already paid in full. Two rooms with an adjoining door. Are you on your honeymoon?'

Rose smiled. 'We're not married, and his surname is not Garden, but please don't tell anyone. He's tried to convince me that Kangaroo Island is like Gretna Green, and couples can elope here to be married. I'm checking it out for a friend.'

The young receptionist tapped at her nose. 'I've read about that place in Scotland, but KI is part of South Australia, so the same marriage rules apply.'

Rose signed her form as Rose Garden, and Nic squiggled on his.

'I'm Taylor. Welcome to The Mercure and KI. We have you staying for five nights. Is there anything you'd like to see while you're here?' Rose folded out the road map. 'We're here for the K.P.I. Events at the racecourse. Do you know if it will still be on despite the impending COVID shutdowns?'

'I'm not sure, as you are the first to book here for that. It's supposed to start in two days. The tourist numbers are down because of COVID, but people are still coming over to see what KI is famous for.'

Nic nodded. 'Kangaroos.'

'Nope, the seals and koalas. So, if you're heading down to Flinders Chase, return before dark. The animals get a little crazy.'

'The seals or the koalas?'

'Nope, the kangaroos. They don't understand the road rules and stand still when a car comes at them when it's dark. They get mesmerised by the lights and tend to make a mess of your car if you run into them.' Nic grinned. 'Good to know. We'll have a big day tomorrow and be off to our rooms. Is there anywhere to eat around here?'

'We're open for dinner from six and breakfast from...um...six. Otherwise, you must drive back to the city to get something.'

Rose looked at her. 'I assume you mean Kingscote?'

'Yep, that's the biggest city on the island and the biggest one I've ever been to. I'm only twenty and look forward to attending Adelaide for my twenty-first birthday party. I've heard it's a lot bigger. There's even a shopping mall and everything. You even have to pay if you park on the street.'

Rose and Nic left the receptionist to ponder her future and headed for their rooms.

Rose and Nic were waiting in the breakfast room at six the following day. Only two other couples were present, so Rose started conversing with one of the other guests. 'Are you here for the kangaroos, koalas or seals?' The man looked at her with a blank expression. 'No, we're here for breakfast.'

They were led to their seats. The breakfast menu included the normal fare; everything was listed as locally made, grown, or produced. Nic ordered toast with honey. It, too, was locally made by the Ligurian bee population. Rose hadn't yet ordered, so Nic whispered: 'I dare you to order avocado on toast. They don't grow them on the island.'

Rose ignored him and asked for two poached eggs on toast. Both locally made and produced. They finished breakfast and returned to their rooms when the daily local newspaper, 'The Islander,' was delivered to reception. Rose took a copy.

The main story referred to a female's body found on the beach at Stokes Bay. A fifteen-year-old boy had been using a drone with his phone attached and taking a photograph; then, he called the authorities. There were more pictures inside. No details were provided about who she was and whether she was still alive.

They went into Rose's room, and Nic folded the road map. 'I guess we should get our bearings. See where everything is, that sort of thing. We'll head to the racecourse first, then do some sightseeing.'

Nic returned to his room to wait for Rose to decide what she would wear for the day's adventure. He turned the television on, and the local news channel also showed the story about the unknown woman. They called her 'Jane Doe' but confirmed she was alive and is currently in a coma at Kingscote Hospital. Her condition was considered critical but stable. A television camera crew managed to access the hospital room and filmed the young woman unconscious. Rose entered Nic's room and noticed the vision. 'That's disgusting. They don't even know who she is and if she'll live, yet they are making it into a television show.'

The cameraman focused on the young woman's face, and the presenter stepped closer, holding her head up to get a better close-up. 'Jane Doe. Does anyone know who she is? She was found on the beach at Stokes Bay. No, ID, no, nothing. We do have her phone, though. Maybe we can learn something from that, but they can't unlock it.

What a terrible shame no one is here to claim her. She must be someone's daughter.' Rose shook her head. 'Turn it off, Nic. It's ghoulish.'

Nic pressed the remote, and the television went black. 'OK, Mrs Rose Garden, are you ready to hop about KI?'

'Sure, but I might call Sandy to see how she's feeling.'

Rose stepped outside into the sunshine. 'Hey, how's it going?'

'Good, we're both over the worst of it, but the case numbers are increasing. I won't be surprised if every state goes into lockdown. It's going to kill the economy.' Rose could hear another voice in the background. 'That doesn't sound like your Father. Do you have someone else staying there?' Sandy leaned away from the mouthpiece. 'Dad, can you turn her off? I'm on the phone to Rose.'

The voice in the background suddenly got louder, yelling something about the local news, and Rose couldn't hear anything over the din. Sandy spoke a little louder. 'I'll call you back later. Dad is having trouble with Alexa. He's trying to hook everything into Amazon but hasn't got a handle on how to use it yet.'

'Sure, we might be out of range, though, as the phone coverage here is a little sketchy.'

Rose disconnected and went back inside. Nic had turned the television on again and was watching a golf channel. 'How are Sandy and Robb?'

'Getting better slowly, not like that girl in the hospital.' Rose suddenly realised she'd seen the girl before: 'I...Alexa...her name's Alexa. We met her at the racecourse in Doomben. Sandy and I took a selfie with the horse. I think it's her.' Rose opened her phone, went to the gallery app, and showed it to Nic. 'I think we should go to the Kingscote Hospital.'

Nic nodded. 'Interesting development, Mrs Garden. I'll make a call and see if we can get access to her room.' Nic stepped outside and returned a few moments later. 'I've been told that a detective from Adelaide has been assigned to the case, and she will meet us there at about lunchtime today. Meantime, how about we drive down to the racecourse and see if Charles Carrington The Third has made it over here.' Rose looked at him. 'How did you get all that organised so quickly?'

'I am The Batman.'

29

Around twenty minutes later, Nic and Rose were at the Kangaroo Island Racecourse. A long row of temporary tents was erected adjacent to the finish line, and workers were finalising the advertising banners. There was no mention of the K.P.I Events running the operation. Nic headed for the main auditorium, leaving Rose to approach the workers. 'Hi guys, do you know if the K.P.I. event is still on tomorrow?' The man shrugged and pointed her toward another man holding a folder. It was open, and he wasdirecting the others where to apply the banners.

Rose repeated the question, and the man looked at her. 'I don't know, but there ain't going to be a race of anything unless the horses and dogs get here. Last I heard, no one's sending them over due to COVID. They going to lose a motza.' Rose nodded. 'Is Charles Carrington around? Have you seen him?'

The man looked at her with a puzzled expression. 'What do you want him for?'

'We met him in Brisbane, it's his event. He's putting it on. K.P.I Events.'

'No, it's not. They wouldn't allow an outsider here. It would do the track out of any takings. You're wrong, lady, he's putting you on. Now leave, I've got to get this stuff done.' The foreman barked to a couple of lads vaping. 'Stop that, I don't pay you to stand around smoking.' One of the lads gave him the middle finger salute. 'We're not smoking, we're vaping. There's a difference.'

Rose left the area and headed towards the auditorium to locate Nic. She noticed a young woman with a Doomben Racecourse windcheater emblazoned across the front. The girl looked about ten years old. 'Hi, I'm Rose. Have you come all the way down from Brisbane?' The young girl glanced at her, and Rose continued: 'Your windcheater. It says 'Doomben'. I was there recently; we met Alexa. Do you know her?' The girl started to cry. 'I...yes...she's my sister, but I don't know where she is. She's gone missing. I saw her get into a car with the boss-man and I haven't seen her since. She's supposed to be here helping me.'

Rose opened the app on her phone. 'Is this Alexa?'

The girl nodded. 'Yes, how did you get that? She doesn't like having her photo taken.'

Rose sighed. 'Have you seen the local newspaper or heard the news lately? A young woman was found on the beach at Stokes Bay. She's in a coma at Kingscote Hospital.'

'Oh, my God. Is she all right?'

'Well, she's in a coma.'

'Oh, my God...but is she all right?'

'I'm here with my friend. Would you like to come with us to the hospital? We are meeting with a Detective they've sent from Adelaide to investigate.'

The girl looked at Rose. 'Was she bashed up or anything?'

'They haven't said, only that she's in a coma.'

'Was she drugged?'

Rose looked at her. 'I think you should come with me, and we'll find my friend. As I said, I'm Rose. What's your name?'

'You'll laugh. Please don't laugh. It's Cortana Case. My parents named us both after those silly AI computer thingy's.'

'Why would I laugh? My name is Rose Garden.'

Cortana smiled. 'Hey, that's worse than my name.'

The girl put her hand into Rose's, and they moved towards the auditorium. Rose noticed that Nic was talking to Carrington, and Cortana stepped back behind her so she couldn't be seen. 'He's the bad man that took Alexa.'

Rose stepped back outside and rang Nic. Carrington stepped away, and Nic took the call. 'It's Rose. I'm standing outside with Cortana, she's Alexa's sister.'

Nic nodded and came outside to meet her. 'Hi Cortana, I'm Nic.'

'Do you have a funny name too, Mr Nic?'

Nic smiled. 'Nope, just Nic. Did Rose tell you about Alexa?'

'Yes. She's sick in the hospital. That man you were talking to made her sick.'

'Sorry, Cortana, he told me he hasn't seen her since you came on the ferry.'

'He's a big fat liar, and his pants are on fire.'

Nic smiled. 'Are you here with your parents?'

'Nope. Alexa is my um...she looks after me. My guardian, she's over eighteen. Our parents died in a car crash last year. Alexa says that that man had nothing to do with it, but I don't think that. He's a liar.' Cortana started to cry again.

Rose hugged her. 'Are you able to tell me where they had their accident?' The girl took a sniff. 'It was near the big red rock, in the middle of Australia; they hit a big red kangaroo with their little red Porsche Boxter car.' Rose looked to Nic, and they realised the matter wasn't worth pursuing.

'Would you like to come with us to the hospital?'

'I can't.'

'Why?'

'I'm not allowed to get into cars with strangers. Alexa told me that. I don't know who you are, and she cannot tell me it's OK.'

Nic smiled. 'What if I told you I was with the Police?'

Cortana sniffed again. 'Are you a Policeman?'

'Not quite, but I'm friends with the Police Commissioner of South Australia. He's the man in charge of all the Police. I can ring him, and he'll say it's OK.' Rose looked at Nic. 'That won't work, Nic. Cortana doesn't know him either. We'll have to leave Cortana here until it gets sorted out.'

Rose looked down at the child. 'Where are you staying now?'

'We are sleeping in a horse float. It's a double bunk. I've got the top bed.'

Nic continued: 'Is anyone else in there with you?'

'Yes, Nancy.'

'Can we speak to her?'

'I don't think so; she's a horse.'

Nic looked over at Rose. 'Your turn.'

Rose squatted down. 'Cortana, who has been looking after you while Alexa has been missing?' The girl nodded. 'Mr Bow Bow. He's the big man holding the folder over there. He likes to yell a lot.'

Rose held out her hand, took Cortana's, moved off to find Mr Bow Bow and located him inside a tent, smoking a cigarette. He butted it out on the ground as they approached him. 'What she's done now?'

Nic held out his hand, and the man reluctantly shook it. 'I'm Nic, and this is Rose. We're investigating the assault on Alexa.'

'I don't know anything about anything.'

Rose looked at him. 'Have you been looking after Cortana while Alexa's been missing?' Mr Bow Bow glared at her. 'Of course, but I've nothing to do with anything else.' Rose raised her voice this time. 'Well, you know something about something; otherwise, Cortana wouldn't need looking after.'

The man took a step backward. 'I guess so. What's happened to Alexa?' Rose continued: 'She was found at Stokes Bay, unconscious on the beach, and now in a coma at Kingscote Hospital. Haven't you seen the news?'

'Nope. Been too busy setting this up.' He held his arms out to show them, and Rose noticed the tattoos on his forearms, they read "Beau and Bow" and realised it was the same man she'd met at the Doomben Racecourse. 'We are about to meet with a Detective they've sent over from Adelaide to investigate it. Can we take Cortana with us to the hospital?'

The man shook his head. 'I'm sorry, I won't allow Cortana to get into the car with strangers.' He then held out his hand, and Cortana took it. 'Are you thirsty? How about we get you a drink, little lady.' They moved off, holding hands.

The dynamic duo returned to the car, and Nic started singing The Doors song: *'People are strange. When you're a stranger.'* Rose looked over at him. 'I've always relied on the strangeness of kinders.'

Nic started up the car. 'What is that from?'

'Palmer, Rose Palmer. I will write my book of mixed-up sayings one day, so I don't have to listen to your idioms. Anyway, did you happen to notice the tattoo on the big guy's arms?'

Nic nodded. 'Yep.'

'And?'

'I would say he's part of Carrington's posse. So we need to be careful.'

30

The drive to Kingscote took around ten minutes, they parked outside the hospital and sat there waiting for the Detective. Nic's phone pinged with a message: 'Behind you.' Nic stepped out of the car and met with the Detective.

'Good to see you again, Nic. It's been a while since we worked together. How is Sister Gwen? Has she recovered yet?'

Nic smiled. 'Nope, as crazy as ever, and speaking of crazy, let me introduce you to Rose, she's my latest and greatest associate.'

Rose held out her hand. 'Hi, I'm Rose.'

The Detective shook her hand, nodded, and smiled. 'I know, you took my job.' Rose stepped back and looked at Nic. 'You told me you only work alone?'

'Yep, I work alone, but I work alone with you and Sandy and Chewy and all the Drivers, and the Police and sometimes with my Father.'

The Detective looked at Nic. 'You've never worked with your Father.' The Detective faced Rose. 'I'm Senior Detective Fletcher Chastain, but call me 'Fletch,' everybody does. I've got the vision from the lad that found her. It's quite short. He was up on the ridge above the bay and saw what he thought was a seal on the beach, so he zoomed the drone down to look closer. It was the young woman. Let's go inside and find an office we can use.'

Rose whispered, 'Alexa Case' as they entered the hospital entrance. 'Her name is Alexa Case, we met her younger sister, Cortana, at the racecourse.'

They stepped into an office, and Fletch set up her laptop. 'Do you know her?'

'No, Sandy and I happened to take a selfie with her at Doomben when we met Carrington. I recognised her face from the television.'

Fletch nodded. 'Good job. Now we have a who, let's work out the why. Here's the vision.' She pressed 'enter'. 'I've already looked at it. There's only one set of footprints in the sand, so I have no idea how or if she was assaulted. I spoke to the lad, and he saw no one else on the beach. It's a mystery.'

They watched the vision through three times and were none the wiser. Nic nodded. 'There's nothing there. Have the results come back from the bloods yet?'

'We have to talk to the Doctor about that. He rang me as he found something interesting but wouldn't tell me over the phone.'

A knock was on the door, and a young intern stepped in. 'I'm Doctor Pride. You've been waiting for me.' Fletch nodded. 'Yes, thanks for coming in. This is Nic and Rose; they're helping me with the investigation. What do you know?'

'She was assaulted. I found minute traces of wood and silver on her skull. The bloods showed that she'd been drugged.' The Doctor referred to his notes. 'The choice of drug was Ketamine, with an additional dose of Midazolam.'

Fletch whistled. 'Short term. Ketamine would make her dizzy, but the other shouldn't keep her unconscious.'

'Oh, no. We did that. The television crew kept hanging around trying to get an interview with her, so we kept her doped up to stop them from making it into a media circus. She's conscious now.'

Rose googled both drugs. 'Ketamine is used on horses; they use the other one as an anaesthetic.' The Doctor nodded. 'Yes, whoever did this was either interrupted or stupid. Neither of the drugs would kill her if that were their intent. The dosage would have to be high, and you couldn't carry it around in a syringe.'

Nic nodded. 'Can we speak to her?'

'Sure. I'll show you where she is.' The Doctor led the group along the passageway and opened the door to the ward. 'Um...that's not good.'

Fletch looked in. 'Why.'

'She's gone.' The Doctor returned to the passage and called out: 'Code Black Alpha...um...Code Yellow...um ...What colour is a missing patient?' A Nurse called out. 'There's isn't one yet, but someone just came in and asked me why a gurney was in the middle of the road.'

Nic, Rose and Fletch ran outside, but the street was empty. Fletch stopped. 'Where's your car? I took a taxi.'

Rose pointed to the carpark. 'It's the Karmann Ghia. It's got a back seat. Why?'

'We need to go to Stokes Bay to find out what happened. I reckon we have about three hours of daylight.'

'What about Alexa?'

"Whoever has her can't get off the island. They've shut the ferry service and closed the airport due to the COVID pandemic.'

Rose was driving, Fletch sat in the passenger seat and Nic sat in the back. They drove off towards Stokes Bay. Fletch folded out the road map. 'Take the high road and head for Parndana along the Playford Highway, then we turn right into Stokes Bay Road. It's about a forty-minute drive.'

Nic was bouncing around in the back seat, and his phone rang. 'Yep, Interesting, thanks, Chewy.' He disconnected. 'Chewy found out Carrington is staying at The Cottages in Stokes Bay. He rang them and told them he was with the Police. They'll call you if he turns up.'

Fletch turned around. 'So why do you think it's him?'

'He's got access to Ketamine and probably the other drug, and when I asked him what happened to his cane, he told me he'd broken it, so threw it away. He told me he's paid well over a thousand dollars for it.'

Rose interjected. 'And there's the small issue of the scam he was pulling here.'

'What scam?'

'Chewy and I have been researching the event. It turns out he's tried something similar before but didn't get away with it. The event was abandoned due to excessive rainfall, in this case, it's COVID.' Fletch pointed to the upcoming right-hand turn, and Rose took it, doing about seventy.

Nic called out from the backseat. 'The speed limit here is only sixty, Rose.'

Rose shook her head. 'We've got the sirens on.' Rose pressed the horn, and it gave a little beep. 'Besides, the car is red, which must mean something otherwise why do they paint Fire Engines red?'

They arrived at the Cottages, and Fletch went inside with her badge held up, then returned a few moments later. 'He's not here, but they told me he'd just driven past and saw someone was in the passenger seat with him. Let's go to the beach.'

Nic nodded. 'He's probably driving a white Holden Statesman. Rego 'Bravo India Golf, Whisky India Golf.' Big-Wig. The Chief Racecourse Steward owns it and has just reported it stolen.'

The trio drove to the beach and leaped out of the car. The Statesman was parked in the area, but it was empty. Fletch looked around. 'Where can they go?'

Rose nodded. 'Back to the scene of the crime perhaps?' Nic and Fletch took off towards the high trail. It would take them along the ridge where the lad had been standing with his drone.

Rose took a breath and called out to them. Sorry, I didn't bring my running shoes,' and sat back in the car, trying to get a signal on her phone. It wasn't working, so she decided to take a walk around. She could see Nic and Fletch scrambling along the ridge path. Rose sat down in the shed provided for sun shelter, sipping on a bottle of water and reading the signs about the local area's history when an elderly couple surprised her. 'Where did you come from?'

The old man grinned. 'Through the rocks. They built a pass through the rocks that take you through to Hidden Beach. It's so beautiful over there. No seaweed, just golden sand. There's only one other couple over there now, but she doesn't look at all well.' Rose looked at him, then recalled the vision from the lad's camera. It was a different view. It wasn't the same beach that sprawled out in front of her. 'How do you get there?'

'Just follow the path and the footsteps in the sand. Don't think about it. Just believe. The path will lead the way.'

The couple left, so Rose took her shoes off, entered the gap in the rock wall and followed the footprints in the sand. After a five minute trek, noticed the path stopped at a rock face and Rose recalled what the old man had said: *Follow the footsteps in the sand. The path will lead the way.'*

Rose ignored her brain, telling her there was no point in proceeding further and followed the footprints, which led her through a slender cut-out between two rock walls. Rose stepped onto the beach into the afternoon sunshine.

Nic and Fletch were nowhere to be seen, but Carrington was there with Alexa so called out to him. 'Stop, Carrington. It's over. Nic and Senior Detective Fletcher Chastain are on the ridge above us, and the Police are on their way. Let her go.' Carrington stopped, but he didn't turn around, however, he let go of Alexa, and she flopped onto the beach sand. Carrington then started to jog away.

Rose carefully approached Alexa so as not to startle her and the young woman's eyes fluttered open. 'Hi Alexa. We met at Doomben. I'm Rose, and Cortana says hello.' Rose cradled her head and offered her a drink of water.

Alexa smiled up at her. 'I thought I was going to die out here the other day. I told him I knew everything about the scam with the horses, the dogs, and the everything. He hit me with his cane, then drugged me with something.'

'We know, but how did he get you through the gap in the rocks the other day?'

Alexa took a breath. 'I met him on this side of the beach. I came over the ridge. I didn't know about the rock wall tunnel thing. He snuck up behind me and smashed me over the head with his cane. I thought I was going to die.'

Alexa took another breath. 'How is Cortana?'

'She's fine. Mr Bow Bow is looking after him. Do you feel well enough to walk back through the rock tunnel?'

'I think so. I'm a bit fuzzy, though. What drug did he give me?'

'Ketamine, but in hospital, they had you in an induced coma to keep the prying media away.' Alexa grinned, 'Oh, OK. So...OK...they want a story, do they? Have I got a good one for them?' Rose assisted Alexa in rising, and they slowly returned through the rock tunnel to the car.

About half an hour later, Nic, Fletch and a very unhappy Charles Carrington The Third, who was now wearing a lovely pair of silver handcuffs, approached Rose and Alexa sitting in the car. Rose stepped out. 'You found him then.'

Nic smiled. 'Yep, and we brought him back through the hole in the wall. Did you know that...' but before Nic could finish, Rose whispered. 'Yep, but let's keep it our little secret, and I know how bad you are at keeping those.'

They bundled Carrington into the Statesman, and Nic drove with Fletch back to the Kingscote Police Station to formalise the arrest. Rose led Alexa to the Carmen Ghia and returned to racecourse. They met with Cortana, collected their belongings, and then drove to the Mercure at American River. Rose booked them into a room and Alexa couldn't believe her generosity. 'Why are you putting us in the Hotel? How long are we here? We should get back to the racecourse.'

'It's called recuperating, Alexa, and after what you've been through, it's the least we can do. You're both here for as long as it takes.'

Rose handed over one of Nic's business cards, opened the door and showed them in. Cortana ran inside and jumped up and down on the bed. 'I've got my own bed and everything, and look, we've even got a bathroom with a shower and everything.

We won't have to wash in the same water as Nancy, and there's a television, too.'

Rose left them to rest, returned to her room and called Nic. 'Can you talk?'

'Yep, just let me go outside.' Rose waited, and Nic came back onto the call. 'Are they settled in? How did it go?'

'Alexa and Cortana wanted to know why they'd be hiding out at the Mercure and how long they could stay.'

Nic nodded. 'What did you say?'

'I told them to stay as long as they wanted to. I'll go to the reception a bit later and organise some things for them to see on KI if anything stays open with this COVID thing.'

'Sounds like a plan. Alexa will most likely have to testify against Carrington about the scam he was pulling, but from what Fletch said, he's stuck in jail here for a while anyway. She'd been collating stuff about his scam, so he won't even get bail at this stage. I hope he likes staring out the windows at the kangaroos.'

Rose smiled. 'So are we heading back to Adelaide or home to Brisbane? I assume we'll have to leave the car on KI, and they've closed the ferry service. Robb will have to collect it later when they open the ferry service.'

'Yep, I've already set that up with Sandy. Anyway, now about the news. There's some bad news and some good news. Which do you want first, as there are a few parts to it.'

'Just the news.'

'Well, the good news is that we can get back to Brisbane, so the second part of the good news is we're flying back.'

'And I assume you're the pilot?'

'Yep.'

'Damn you, Nic. Will you be here later tonight for dinner?'

'Yep, and bring along the others too if they're not too tired of sleeping.'

31

Fletch and Nic drove back to the Mercure and met with the others in the Dining Room. They ordered meals, and Fletch withdrew a small leather pouch from her jacket. 'I'm sorry, Alexa, but there are just a few more details I need to run through with you before I leave. Here's your phone. I collected it from the hospital.' Alexa nodded. 'Did you get everything off it that you needed?'

Fletch smiled. 'And a whole lot more. Carrington was co-ordinating it all. It's a very elaborate scam, and thanks to you, we've stopped him in his tracks.' Fletch looked over at Rose. 'It was going to be his show, his bookies, his horses, and his jockeys. Everything was rigged to make him a lot of money, in the millions, if he was successful. He even ensured first access to the photo finish camera in case it came to that. This was simply a way for him and his cronies to rip off unsuspecting punters. We've put a stop to all of it.'

Nic leaned forward. 'It all came crashing down because of Alexa.'

Alexa smiled. 'I almost got killed and I don't know if I'll ever be able to work in the industry again. Everybody will know what I did. It won't take long for the word to get around. It's going to be tough for me and Cortana.'

Fletch smiled and handed over two New Zealand passports. 'Have you ever heard of the Witness Protection Programme? You'll be leaving KI tomorrow morning and catching an International flight from Brisbane to Auckland later this evening. It's the last one before they close the borders. A Detective will collect you at the airport and fly you down to Christchurch the following day.'

Alexa looked stunned. 'Both of us?' Alexa opened the passports and looked at the pictures. 'This is a recent photo of me; where did you get it from? I've been avoiding getting my photo taken.' Rose opened the app on her phone and showed her. 'This is how I knew who you were. We took it at Doomben.'

Alexa smiled. 'Nice horse.'

Fletch pointed to the names in the passports: 'You're now Alexandra Boxter and Cortney Boxter. That should keep you safe. We'll contact you when the trial begins, but most likely, you won't have to come back over the ditch for it.'

This time Nic nodded in confirmation. 'And here are your airline tickets to Auckland. Rose can teach you how to speak 'Long White Cloud,' as her Mother came from over there.'

Rose smiled. 'You'll be OK. They speak English.'

Alexa handed Cortana her passport. 'We're going on a holiday to New Zealand for a while…um…Cortney.'

Cortana looked over at her. 'Can Nancy come too?'

Alexa was trying to back her tears, then smiled. 'Sorry, kiddo, we're on our own again.' She looked at Fletch. 'I had no idea what the future held for us. Our Grannies and Pops died before I was born, and now all of this…thank you.' Fletch held her hand. 'No, thank you, Alexandra.'

The following day Nic, Rose, Alexa and Cortana were waiting for clearance to fly at the KI airport. Cortana was sitting in the co-pilot seat while Rose and Alexa sat on the luxurious leather couches. They buckled in and Rose poured some drinks. Rose leaned over. 'Sorry, Alexa, it looks like you didn't see much of KI, but you'll enjoy Christchurch as they have a great University there. We've enrolled you to study Veterinary Science, and the Uni is the best in New Zealand. It's a great town to grow up in, and Cortana…sorry, Cortney, will love it too.'

Nic tapped at his microphone to tell the others they were about to take off. *'This is Tango Victor. Seeking clearance to fly.'* Nic leaned over to Cortana. 'Hold on; we're about to take off.'

'Roger Tango Victor. You're the only flight out today, so look to avoid the kangaroos on the runway. Enjoy the Cirrus Vision Jet. The new owner will meet you in Brisbane in about four hours.'

As the plane has a flight speed of around five hundred kilometres an hour, there wasn't much time for Rose to be concerned about the flight or the crashing or anything much at all, apart from watching out the window as Australia zoomed past underneath them. They landed safely, and Nic handed over the keys.

A Senior Detective met with the group and escorted his two young passengers to the Air New Zealand lounge. Nic and Rose watched the plane depart, then hailed a taxi and headed home. 'That was some adventure, Rose. I bet Carrington was hopping mad he got caught and he'll be yelling at everyone to let him out. I hope it makes him a little hoarse.'

Rose was about to respond when her phone rang. She held up her finger and stepped away from him to take the call. It was her mother, Jana, and she blurted out: 'Your Father is being charged with cryptocurrency fraud. I don't even know what that means.' Her Mother abruptly hung up.

<u>Dedication</u>

'I felt like Miranda when I passed through that rock.'

'That was an Aussie film from '75. The story was made up.'

'I thought you didn't believe in making up stories, Nic.'

<u>Introducing Book 8 in the Nic Thorn Caper series:
Eight Dave's are Weak.</u>

Rosemary Palmer was surrounded by stuff, but it wasn't the good stuff between chocolate macaroon cupcakes, it was the stuff you find in the remnants of dead computers. Rose picked up a motherboard and tossed it into the box labelled "Motherboards," however, the next piece of hardware was a little more challenging, as it was a tiny flat plastic box with protruding wires. It looked like a dead centipede.

Rose referred to the list she had been provided, where each piece had been hand-drawn and labelled accordingly, and considered where to put it. Nic Thorn, Rose's friend, mentor, and scam-busting associate, entered the room holding another box of the crunchy, crushed computer bits and dropped it on the table. 'What have you found?'

Rose picked up the crushed piece of computer candy and was about to suggest where he could put the next box when her phone rang. Swiping upwards, there was silence at the other end of the telephone, so she re-read the number and confirmed it was her mother, Jana, calling and she was hyper-ventilating between loud sobs:

'They've taken your Father off to jail. He's been arrested for his involvement in a cryptocurrency fraud. Whatever that means.'

Nic overheard the comment and moved closer so then Rose used her finger to cover the mouthpiece: 'Apparently, my Father has been taken off to jail.'

Rose finally broke into the conversation. 'It will work out, whatever it is, Mother, as long as no one has died. Has some-one died?'

Jana then took a loud gulp of air. 'No, Rosemary, but that's not the point.'

Rose sighed, then added. 'Unless *he* killed someone, and I haven't heard anything regarding that.'

Jana slowed down. 'No, he hasn't, he didn't, but he's...they came and took him away. He was handcuffed, and the whole street watched as they put into the backseat of the Police Car. It was so embarrassing.'

'What time was this?'

'About three this afternoon. It was right in the middle of the school run. Everyone stopped to see what was going on. I rang Mr Wonderful, Michael. He said not to worry about it.'

Rose sighed heavily at the mention of her ex-husband. Rose was required to marry Michael due to a stern directive from her father to win over a business deal. The marriage lasted three very long days, and the business deal didn't last much longer. Although over ten years ago, Rose still struggles to come to terms with it. 'Mother, please stop calling him that. Was Michael arrested too?'

Jana took a breath. 'No, Rosemary. Why would you expect that? He's a wonderful man, and I hope one day you'll see what you missed out on by not staying married to him.' Rose did a mental head-slap. 'What did Michael tell you? Is he going to the Police Station to talk to them?'

'No, not at all. Why would he be doing that?'

'You said Father had been arrested for fraud, Michael is his Accountant.'

F or more reading from the Nic Thorn and Rose Palmer Series of capers:

<u>One Tricked Phoney</u>

Rose needed a +1, but not for the usual wedding/party. She
was going to a funeral and needed a quiet, unassuming type.
The best option was to use her dating site, but when Nic
Thorn arrived, he was anything but a wallflower. Their very
first adventure leads them from one lively caper to another,
this time involving portrait provenance, invoice inaccuracy,
and a recycler's relapse, on their travels from Brisbane, Adelaide, to the SA border.

<u>Two hurtled Gloves</u>

Rose Palmer was to be a bride again, but this time, Nic
Thorn ensured it wasn't the short, fat and shallow man her
parents forced her to marry the first time. Together with her
BFF Sandy, they move onto another tale, this one tracking
down the elusive and believed to be extinct Thylacine. Sandy
loses her identity, and Nic introduces them to the benign
world of banking, but there is much more involved when the
loan arranger is unmasked as a fraud.

<u>Three French Bens</u>

Nic's friend, Benoit Trudeau, is one-third of the 'Three
French Bens'. He has just bought into a high-end restaurant,
so he called Nic's Team in to have a look, as the numbers look
fishy, and they might have to go angling for the truth. Nic
and his crew then head to Rockhampton to help the Queens-
land Department of Agriculture inspect some cattle duffing

and Sandy has to deal with an old school friend, or is that a fiend lending to her at her expense?

<u>Four Brooding Birds</u>

The Australian Department of Agriculture often deals with sneaks and adders, and this time, Nic and the team are brought in to investigate reptile smuggling. Lizards have been discovered stuffed into a women's singlet, and her accomplice is caught with his own jocks of frogs, but they deny any knowledge of how they got in there. Then the team tries to drink from the sweet success of wines, but it turns out to be someone who can't stop whining about how he has to keep everything bottled up inside and to complete their investigation they have to look into genuine budgie smugglers.

<u>Five Mouldy Bins</u>

It's Christmas in July, and the Department of Health in Brisbane is concerned that someone may be stuffing their mattress with ill-gotten gains, so Nic and the team are brought in to bring it to a head – reindeer style. Sandy and Rose meet up with their 'friend' Dimond, who keeps handing over her hard-earned money to lease a new rental property for her husband and family as it turns out the Real Estate Agent knows how to manage to take the deposit too, but only ever in cash. Then, the team gets involved in a diamond scam. The resolution could be clear cut, but getting stranded in Dubai on the way to South Africa was never in the plan.

<u>Six Geezers Lying</u>

Car insurance companies are driven up the wall by bogus claims and 'accidents'. It's about time someone gives the scammers a crash course on how to stop. Then, one of the national restaurant chains puts together a competition so easy that anyone can win, but what happens when the prizes are won before the contest is finished? The team then gets involved in an art scam, and Rose's Father is in the middle of it. Art is not always art but scamming is always fraud.